Once Upon a Time in Junior High

Once Upon a Time in Junior High

Lisa Norment

AN
APPLE
PAPERBACK

SCHOLASTIC INC.
New York Toronto London Auckland Sydney

ISBN 0-590-45287-8

12 11 10 9 8 7 6 5 4 3 2 1   4 5 6 7 8 9/10

Printed in the U.S.A.   40

First Scholastic printing, January 1994

For my family:
William, Eleanor, Denyce, Ricky,
Tony, Tiffany, and Krystina

Once Upon a Time in Junior High

1

There are eighteen Anderson families listed in the Brookeville phone directory, and I personally know two of them. One of the Anderson families includes my best friend, Shelby, her dad, mom, and younger sister, Paige. The other Anderson family includes Daddy, Ma, my older sister, Alexandra, and me, Amber. My family is listed before Shelby's because my dad's name is Phillip. Shelby's dad is Robert.

I know it's stupid, but every spring when the new directory comes out, Shelby and I love to examine our family names in it. We think it's so cool that we both have the same last name, even though we're not related!

"Anderson-comma-Phillip-and-Justine," I quote, "one sixty-two Foxhill Road."

Shelby and I always giggle at the never-changing entry, then she will thumb down exactly four names and read, "Anderson-comma-Robert-and-

Diane, two-twelve Foxhill Road. Same as always."

Shelby's lived in Brookeville all of her life. I used to live in Queens. One day about four years ago, I got home from Thomas Jefferson Elementary School, and Ma said, "Amber, pull out your suitcases, we're moving." I thought it was a joke, but she was serious. The next week we moved and we've lived at 162 Foxhill Road ever since.

For some weird reason, it makes me feel better to know our names are in that directory. Seeing Phillip and Justine listed lets me know I'll always have my family. And because Robert and Diane are just a few listings down, I know I'll always have Shelby.

"Connery, Connolly, Connolly, Connor, Connors."

"Wait!" Shelby interrupted me as I read through the directory. "You just skipped it."

She frantically grabbed the directory from my hands, and demanded, "Where is it?"

"It" was the listing for Stephen and Pauline Connor, parents of the hunk of Brookeville Junior High, Patrick Connor. Or as Shelby would correct, "Patrick *Gilbert* Connor." Anyway, at least half of the Brookeville female population (under the age of fourteen) was in love with him, including, unfortunately, Shelby.

So, on the last official day of summer vacation we sat and searched for a listing for Patrick *Gil-*

2

bert Connor in the now crumpled, grease-stained white pages of the Brookeville telephone directory. As far as I could remember, this was the only other time I had so much as opened the directory since last spring when Shelby and I had our annual ritual of looking up our own names.

"I don't see it," Shelby whined. "You've lost the page." Shelby was beginning to get into one of her baby moods, the kind where if I were to get into one, Ma would tell me, "Oh, whining like a baby won't do anybody any good."

But I didn't say this to Shelby. Instead I decided to whine back, "Well, you snatched it out of my hands!"

"Because you wouldn't give it to me," Shelby insisted.

"Oh, *re*lax!" I was getting annoyed because I'd had enough of hearing about Patrick Connor this summer to bug any normal twelve-year-old to death.

"We can find it again," I sighed.

Shelby really had it bad. She was in love with someone she didn't have a chance in the world with, at least as far as I was concerned.

A couple of weeks ago, Shelby and I were walking back from Sidney's Grocery Store, our arms loaded with bags filled with the ingredients for a new recipe we were going to try. Somehow, Shelby and I managed to trip over each other's feet, and before we knew what hit us, we both ended up on our butts, right in the middle of the sidewalk. At first I felt nothing but the pain in my behind, and then I saw the face Shelby made when she hit the ground right after I did. The tomatoes I had been carrying rolled down the sidewalk, and the carrots had flown out of Shelby's bag and landed in the bushes. I couldn't help but ignore my aching bottom and laugh at the whole scene.

Shelby joined me. We laughed and laughed like two idiots, until we saw who was running over to help us.

Decked out in white tennis shorts and a T-shirt was Patrick Connor himself! Shelby almost died, right there on the sidewalk.

"Hey." He smiled with one corner of his mouth. "You guys okay?"

"Yeah," I calmed down enough to choke out, "I guess so. Shelby?"

By then, Shelby was trying to make the moment seem dignified. She grinned stupidly at Patrick and answered in a squeaky voice, "Um — yeah, I'm okay. Thanks."

From that day on, Shelby declared him to be "the god of the century," and has unsuccessfully tried to intrigue him ever since. That's why we'd spent the entire summer investigating this guy. Shelby's goal was to "have" a boyfriend by the end of summer vacation, and she decided Patrick *had* to be the one. All of her determination and hard work aside — she had exactly nine hours to go.

I jokingly reminded her of her deadline. She smiled and nervously said that she was just going to have to call him up.

"That's stupid," I warned.

"Why?" demanded my poor lovestruck friend.

"Well, first of all, he's going to be a hot-shot eighth-grader this year," I reasoned.

"So?" Shelby was not going to give up.

"And you'll just be a lowly seventh-grader." I was desperately trying to save my best friend's feelings, but there was no stopping Shelby.

"Well, it won't hurt for me to call him," Shelby tried to convince herself, "just to say hi."

So, I gave in to Shelby this time, even though I knew her efforts would be a waste of *our* time. But Shelby was my best friend, and if she felt she knew what she was doing, I was just going to have to stick by her.

"You look it up," Shelby demanded as she stretched out on my bed and looked up at the ceiling. She was probably daydreaming about being Patrick's girlfriend again. She had been having these pretty crazy fantasies all summer. Mostly they were about her and Patrick walking down the street holding hands, or riding bikes together, and even *kissing*. Gross! The funny thing was that Shelby had never even held hands with a boy before — let alone *kissed* one!

"Pay attention, Shel," I insisted. "Get a pen so you can write down the number." Shelby, in her dream mode, practically floated across the room humming some unfamiliar tune, and searched in my junky desk drawer for a pen.

When she found one, she used it as a pretend microphone and sang a chorus of, *"La da da da da do do do do do-o-o-o,"* and swayed to her own tune. I rolled my eyes and got back to my search. When I found the "C" listings in the phone book and began reciting the "C-O-N" entries, Shelby began to sigh dramatically and made me lose the page.

When I found the page again, I took Shelby's microphone, retransformed it into a pen, and circled the Connors' name, address, and phone number.

"Well," I handed Shelby my little hot-pink-and-black phone, "call."

Shelby scratched her round blonde head, then smiled with her teeth clenched, the way she did when she was either uncomfortable, or didn't know what to do next. This time it meant she was chickening out of doing what she had insisted she would do.

"Shelby . . ." I warned.

"Right, right." She finally took the phone. "Read me the number."

"Uh — five, five, five," I squinted to see the

tiny numbers without losing the place, "six, zero, four, nine."

Shelby tapped out the numbers on my phone. I could tell she was nervous by the way she was breathing with her mouth open. Her curly, blonde bangs were hanging into her eyes as she stared down at my pink carpet and concentrated on what she was hearing in the phone.

Finally she sat up straight and said, "Hello? Um, is, P-Patrick Gil — um, I mean Patrick there?" She bobbed her head once, then answered, "Thank you." She looked at me with her huge blue eyes, and mouthed to me, "She's getting him."

Shelby squinched her eyes and pulled her arms tightly to her sides in anticipation. I giggled.

I had to admit, this was fun. I never thought she would have the nerve to really call a boy. *I* could never do it.

"Hi-i-i," Shelby suddenly squealed, with this tiny high-pitched voice that sounded more like a hamster than my friend, Shelby.

"Wrong number," she managed to squeak out before she slammed down the phone.

We looked at each other, then broke into hysterics.

"What happened, silly?" I asked when we had calmed down enough to speak.

"It was him." She grinned. "He said, 'Hel-lo.' "

She deepened her voice and tried to sound like Patrick.

We broke into hysterics again and started jumping around. "So why didn't you talk to him?" I asked.

"Because," she sighed, "he sounded too cute!"

"Tell me how he said it again," I pleaded. I was catching what Shelby and I used to call the "silly goose cold." That's when you can't stop laughing. Both Shelby and I had it bad.

"He said, 'Hel-lo.' " She repeated the gruff response.

Of course this set us off again until Ma came into my room and told us to calm down because she could hear us all the way down the hall. After she left, Shelby fell onto my bed and stared at the ceiling again.

"What am I going to do, Amber? I really want him to be my boyfriend," she insisted. "Especially since we'll all be going to the same school."

"Shel, forget him," I sighed. "He's too far out of reach."

Shelby looked serious for a moment. "I guess you're right. Who am I anyway to think someone like Patrick would give me a second thought?"

"Shelby, I didn't mean it like that."

"Besides," Shelby sat back up, ignoring my attempted apology, "we're going to be too busy checking out the seventh-grade guys to bother

8

with any dumb eighth-graders." She got a mischievous look on her face.

"Yeah," I agreed.

"Yeah-h," Shelby mimicked me, then teased, "we've got to find you a boyfriend, Amber."

"Don't even try it, Shel," I warned. "No setting me up this year." When it came to picking guys for me, Shelby had awful taste. Last year, in the sixth grade, she talked Randall Parks into asking me to the End of the Year dance. He was this short kid with frizzy hair that needed a good combing. Poor Randall. When he finally worked up the nerve to ask me to the dance, I sort of frowned in his face, and answered, "Definitely not!"

When I found out who was behind the whole scheme, I practically disowned Shelby as a friend. But she claimed she was only trying to help, and she thought we would make a cute couple. I just gave her a warning *never* to try that again. She promised, and I was left feeling kind of bad for Randall.

That's why I have to be careful who Shelby decides is on the lookout for me. Besides, Dad and Ma would never let me actually date a boy. They'd probably have a fit if they knew we were using my phone to call Patrick.

The rule in my house is no boyfriends until I'm in high school, like my sister, Alexandra. Alexandra is really pretty, so she has tons of boyfriends. Dad and Ma don't have to worry about any boy wanting to date me until I'm eighteen or nineteen, or at least not until the boys my age start catching up to my height.

Besides, there would be only about ten or so black guys in all of Brookeville Junior High, and out of those ten, only about four would be good-looking, and out of those four, with my luck, none would be interested in me. They would like the cute, tiny girls, with cute, tiny haircuts. Without thinking about it, I reached up to touch my thick, corkscrew-curly hair. I wouldn't change my hair for anything — especially for some dumb boy!

Shelby couldn't sit still for a second. She was so bouncy and cute. I hate to admit this, but sometimes I get so jealous of her. She would have it easy in junior high. Everyone would love her. I probably wouldn't have such an easy time this year. Brookeville Junior High is a big school, but there just aren't that many black families living in Brookeville. Sometimes it makes me feel really different from my friends. Sometimes I can't act the same way about certain things. For example, I could never go around saying that I really did think Patrick Connor was cute, and that I sort of had a crush on him, too. I did feel a little guilty about liking a white guy, but what was so wrong with me liking him? But a lot of people probably wouldn't see it that way. Maybe things would be different in junior high.

These feelings were the only things I kept hidden from Shelby. This was something I just couldn't put into words.

"What-sa-matter?" Shelby had noticed that I'd sorta drifted off.

"Oh," I shrugged, "I was just thinking about junior high."

"You're kind of scared?" She sat down on the floor next to me.

I shrugged again. I didn't really know what was wrong with me.

"*I'm* scared," Shelby admitted. I looked into her eyes and felt like bopping myself on the head for ever feeling jealous of someone as great as Shelby.

She put her arm around my shoulder and said, "Don't worry, Anderson. We're the Anderson twins, and we can conquer anything. We won't let junior high scare us!" She gave me that goofy look she gets when she's trying to cheer me up.

"Anderson and Anderson," she declared, "an unbeatable team."

"Anderson and Anderson," I answered back. She was right. We were a team. We had four solid years of friendship behind us. We'd ended up in the same class together every year since the third grade, we always sat next to each other, and we were usually paired together for school projects. This was because we had the same last name, and the teachers would just go down their alphabetized class list when assigning seats or partners.

11

"They'll probably put our lockers next to each other." I smiled.

"They'd better," Shelby nodded, "or else we'll complain."

We laughed. We laughed and broke into a chorus of "Ebony and Ivory," by Paul McCartney and Stevie Wonder. This was sort of our theme song. It's a song about people getting along and living in harmony. The song is kind of old — my parents had it in their old music collection and I found it one day and played it. It reminded me so much of our friendship that I gave it to Shelby two summers ago as an "I'll miss you" present when I went away to camp. Every once in a while, we'll start to sing it when we get into one of our "mushy" moods.

Tomorrow was the first day of junior high and I was really happy that Shelby would be there with me. We would get through it together. We always did.

2

Junior high was *not* getting off to a terrific start. Shelby and I had quickly discovered that we only had one period together — lunch! Luckily, as we'd expected, our lockers ended up right next to each other. *A. ANDERSON* was taped to locker number eighty-four. *S. ANDERSON* was taped to locker number eighty-five.

"Amber, thank God!" Shelby ran up to me.

"Shelby, hi. I haven't seen you all morning." I was really relieved to see a familiar face.

"This place is enormous!" Shelby looked around frantically, but kept a smile on her face. Her hair, as usual, was all over the place. It's not that long, but still manages to get that "wind-blown" look no matter what.

"Everything goes so fast here." She was breathing hard and wrinkled her nose as she spoke.

"As soon as you get settled into one class, it's time to go to the next." She laughed.

I nodded in agreement. She was right. The two-story building was all windows and stone walls with millions of doors leading to the classrooms. From the outside, it never looked so huge, but today it seemed like an entire shopping mall! I remembered how, for the last four years, I had walked past this place on my way to Deer Run Park Elementary. I had longed to be one of the older kids I saw wearing cool clothes and laughing together in huge groups. And now, here I was, one of the older kids, and I was scared out of my mind.

"I know what you mean," I told Shelby, who kept looking around at the groups of kids walking in and out of the classrooms. The sound of lockers banging shut echoed up and down the main hall.

"I keep getting lost," I whispered.

"Me, too," Shelby whispered back. "You wanna know what I did to save myself from too much embarrassment?" She checked to make sure no one else could hear her. "It took me twenty minutes to get into my dumb locker this morning, so I decided to drag all of my books around the rest of the day so I won't have to fidget with that crazy lock again."

"You're kidding," I laughed. "Shel, you're a riot. Only you would think of that." I turned around and began fidgeting with my own stupid lock, which I also had been having trouble opening all morning. My lock had caused me to be late for both of the classes I'd had earlier that day.

14

"Any cute guys in your classes?" Shelby asked with a sly grin.

"Well . . ." I blew on the frizzy curls that kept tickling my forehead, and tumbling down into my eyes. "None in first-period Spanish, but a couple of possibilities in second-period Science. What about you?"

Before she could answer, a tall, lanky guy with glasses and zits came up to Shelby and said, "Hey, blondie, you new here?"

I could tell Shelby was a little disappointed in the pimples and glasses, but was glad to have been noticed. She looked up at the guy and asked, "Who wants to know?"

Cool, Shelby, I silently praised her, and, at the same time I finally got my locker opened. I listened, nonchalantly.

"Carter Nielson wants to know," he answered. "He's standing over there." The guy sort of jerked his head and behind him stood a kind of cute guy with dark curly hair. Carter Nielson wore a black leather jacket and was leaning against the wall, *very coolly.*

Shelby and I sort of peeked around this lanky guy to catch a better glimpse of Carter. I noticed that Carter also wore an earring. He was staring straight at Shelby.

Shelby did look cute in her new sky-blue mini-dress. She had even worn a little bit of eye shadow. It's weird for me to see Shelby as someone a guy would be interested in because I've known her for so long. I mean, I remember when she was really chubby, with dimpled knees and a round belly. Now, at almost thirteen she was losing the fat in the right places. I could picture her in high school as one of those curvy little blonde cheerleaders I've seen at the high school.

"So," the lanky guy continued, "you interested?" Boy, these junior high guys were really forward. But good old Shelby could take care of herself.

"Nah." She lifted one corner of her top lip and sort of shook her head. "I'm already going out with someone."

Glasses and Zits shrugged his shoulders and walked back to Carter Nielson.

"What's happening now?" Shelby asked. She was facing me and I was facing Carter Nielson and company.

"Well," I tried to be inconspicuous, "I think he's reporting your conversation to that Carter guy."

"And what is that Carter guy doing?" demanded Shelby. "Is he still looking at me?"

I looked again. "Yeah, he's smiling. Now they're both laughing, and they both just turned and walked away."

"Whe-e-e-w!" Shelby sighed.

"Whew!" I returned the sigh, then smiled.

Shelby gave me one of her sneaky grins and said, "I played hard to get."

"Shelby Francis Anderson!" I blurted out. "And I thought you really weren't interested."

"Well," Shelby shrugged, "he *was* sort of cute. But you're right, I wasn't interested. I'm keeping my eyes open for Patrick *Gilbert* Connor. Have you seen him today?"

I rolled my eyes and answered, "No, and I really don't plan on it. I mean, he's in the eighth grade, and I doubt he will be hanging around many seventh-grade classes."

The bell rang and I realized I had to walk all the way to the gym for my next class.

"Oh, no," I panicked, "I've got to go!"

I slammed my locker shut before Shelby had time to start drilling me about Patrick *Gilbert* Connor. But I did catch her saying, "Just keep a look out, will ya?" as I ran down the hall toward the gym.

As I rounded the corner, who should I run into? Not Patrick Connor, but one of his beauty-queen girlfriends. We slammed right into each other.

"Watch it, *girlie!*" she sneered at me. I was tall for my age, but she was a lot taller.

"You people don't own the halls!" she said in a nasty voice. She shoved past me, leaving me with my mouth hanging open from the shock of the bump, and her nasty remark.

17

3

G eesh," I mumbled to the now-emptied hall, "how rude — and who are 'you people'?"

This big place made me dizzy. My head began to ache. I slowed down to keep my balance. I felt like I might pass out. But I had to hurry to the gym! Was I crazy? This was the first day of school, this was *junior high*, I could get detention for being caught in the hall between classes. But I didn't care. I slowed down even more.

I suddenly felt very tired. How could I make it through an entire period of gym? I found a girls' bathroom and went in. I'd wanted to be alone, but as the door closed behind me, I knew it wasn't going to happen. Four other black girls leaned against sinks and sat on the window ledge. Two of them were smoking. They wore really nice clothes but they had on too much eyeliner, and this creepy plum lipstick.

For a moment I just stared at them, partially

from surprise, and partially because I really didn't have to use the bathroom and didn't know what to do next.

"Excuse me, I — " I smiled weakly.

"No problem," one of them said. Another really short girl with lots of curly black hair sort of smiled at me. She had tiny, dark eyes. With the exception of the creepy plum lipstick, I liked her, she seemed okay.

I opened my mouth to say something, but couldn't think of anything. So I headed for the nearest stall and shut the door. I expected them to either laugh at me or say something mean. But they didn't.

Instead, they said something that surprised me.

"She's so cute," someone said. "Is she a seventh-grader?"

"Think so," another answered. "She seemed kind of scared."

"Who wouldn't be scared of you, Sheila?" the first girl said.

"Shut up, Tamara!" yelled Sheila.

"Sh-h-h!" another warned. "Y'all are gonna get us kicked outta here. All I need is a detention on the first day!"

The thought of me getting detention along with them made me jump. I flushed the toilet for no reason and ran out of the stall. I ran some water over my hands without looking at them and turned to leave.

" 'Bye," one of the voices said.

" 'Bye." I turned around and smiled shyly at all of them.

4

I didn't get into trouble for getting to class late. Ms. West, the gym teacher, just waved me into line when I walked in. Another class without Shelby. But I did see two girls who had gone to Deer Run Park with me.

Finally, it was lunch. My stomach growled as I made my way to the cafeteria and stood in the long line. I knew Shelby would be here for lunch, and I couldn't wait to see her. This day had been so long, and I still had to go to four classes!

While I waited to be served, I looked down at the clothes I had worn that day — a cutesy pale pink minidress almost like Shelby's blue one. I had loved the dresses when we picked them out last weekend, but today, compared to all the other kids' outfits, I felt kind of babyish. A lot of people wore baggy jeans and sneakers. Most of the guys wore T-shirts underneath button-down shirts that hung open. Some of the girls wore crazy tights with cowboy boots. There were even a few girls who had shown up in micro-miniskirts and high heels!

I wondered how some of these kids got away with dressing like that. My parents would have a fit! I could hear Daddy now, "Young lady, is it Halloween?"

Ma would be so angry that all she'd do is shake her head and press her lips together in a tight line. I smiled to myself at the thought of my parents' reaction to the way the other kids dressed. I could never get away with it, so I didn't try.

I looked around for Shelby but still didn't see her anywhere. Where was she? All seventh-graders had the same lunch period, so I knew she would have to be there, unless — of course! Just as I got to the food counter, in walks Shelby through the huge cafeteria doors with who? Why, Mr. Patrick *Gilbert* Connor, himself.

There he was. He was tall, with dark curly hair, and looked great, as usual. And there was Shelby — short, blonde, crazy hair, and a blue mini. They were complete opposites as far as looks were concerned, but they did look cute together. I could see that he was laughing, and she was smiling up at him. Wow! She couldn't even say hello to him on the phone yesterday! I was dying for Shelby to tell me what was going on.

"Next!" yelled the lunch-server. The girl behind me gave me a shove to move forward and shot me a dirty look.

"Oh." I stared down at the tray of food the lady put in front of me. "Thanks." I handed her my meal ticket.

Darn that Shelby, I thought as I stood like an idiot in front of the entire cafeteria, I wish she would hurry up! I had no one else to sit with.

Finally, I saw Patrick nod his head to her, and Shelby shyly waved her hand. She was still smiling when she turned around and began walking toward the now-shortened lunch line.

"Shel!" I yelled. "Shelby!"

She finally noticed me and began making her way through the line. I could tell that she was about to burst with excitement. Her cheeks were all red, and her smile got bigger.

"Amber!" she squealed, "guess what?"

I was upset and had to fight to hold back my feelings. But I wanted to hear all about her and Patrick.

"What?" I asked calmly.

"Patrick . . ." She hunched her shoulders together and whispered, "He walked me to the cafeteria just now, did you see us?"

I couldn't stay annoyed at Shelby for very long. I loved seeing my best friend in such a great mood. It was fun. "Yes," I admitted, and joined in her excitement, "I did see. You guys looked *so* cute together!"

"Did we?" Shelby asked uneasily. "He's so tall, and I'm so short and dumpy — "

"Oh, stop it, Shel. You really did make a cute couple," I reassured her. "But how did you get him to walk you here?"

"Well," Shelby grabbed my elbow, and led me to an empty spot at one of the nearby tables, "I was sort of lost, and he helped me find my way." She looked sideways, then continued, "Of course I wasn't *really* lost, but I found out where his locker was, and sort of waited for him to show up. Then I walked up to him, and oh-so-coolly asked, 'Excuse me, but could you point me in the direction of the cafeteria? I'm kind of new, and kind of lost.'"

"Shelby, you sneak!"

"Anyway, he not only pointed me in the direction of the cafeteria, but he offered to walk me here, and here I am!" She looked at the ceiling and grinned as we headed for the nearest table.

"And what were you two talking about for so long?" I wanted to know. I ignored my tray of cold mush.

"Well," Shelby sort of frowned, "I really don't know. I can't even remember." She smiled. "Geesh, I was so nervous, I don't know what I said to him — I hope I didn't sound too stupid!"

"Don't worry," I reassured her, "I'm sure you were Ms. Cool."

Shelby was too excited to eat, so she just went on and on about Patrick, and how he was even cuter when he talked and smiled. While I listened to her, I picked over the disgusting lunch that had been dumped on the slate-blue tray. I was too excited to eat. Wow, Shelby with a boy, I thought.

I told her about my encounter with one of his girlfriends in the hall earlier. Shelby laughed and told me not to worry — the girl was probably just a jerk.

We talked and laughed so much that we had blocked out the crowd of seventh-graders who sat around us. We'd almost forgotten where we were and it wasn't until near the end of the lunch period that I noticed what was going on around us. At first, I didn't understand what was wrong. I just had a funny feeling. Then it came to me. I was the only black person at the table. As a matter of fact, I was the only black person sitting in this area of the cafeteria. I noticed a section right in the middle of the cafeteria where a bunch of black kids were sitting together. I didn't feel weird because of where I was sitting, but the looks I was getting from the other kids at the table bothered me. They were all staring at me.

"Shelby," I interrupted her, "everyone's staring at me."

Shelby sort of frowned, looked confused, and then asked, "What are you talking about, Amber?" She looked around the table. "Nobody's staring at you."

But they were. There was no mistaking that half of the table was whispering and nudging each other. I was getting really mad. I felt like standing up and asking, "What in the world are you looking at? Haven't you ever seen two people talking before?" But of course I didn't.

Shelby shrugged, unconvinced, and repeated, "No one's looking at you, Amber."

Shelby took a mouthful of the cold, mushy food from my lunch tray and made a face. "Ewwwww!" she shuddered. "Gross. I think I'll be bringing a bag lunch to school."

"Me, too," I agreed. I couldn't believe they expected us to eat this stuff.

"Yuck, cafeteria food!" I mashed the goo on my tray even more and added, "Yuck, junior high!"

"Yuck!" Shelby agreed.

"YUCK!" we yelled together, and really gave those other kids something to stare at.

"Protest!" Shelby banged her fist on our end of the table.

"Sit-in," I added.

"We'll sit-in at the cafeteria until they serve us human food!" Shelby made me start laughing, and once I started, I couldn't stop. We were acting crazy. We were having fun. The whole table was watching for sure now! But we didn't care!

Just to make certain everyone knew who we were, and to show them we weren't embarrassed, I looked them straight in the eyes and introduced myself, "My name is Amber Felice Anderson, and I am protesting!"

Shelby followed my lead and stated, "And I am Shelby Francis Anderson, and I am protesting — would anyone like to join us?" That made us laugh even harder. I couldn't believe we were doing this in front of a table of strangers. They looked at us like we were from another planet. I only recognized two people from Deer Run Park. They pretended not to know us.

The bell rang. Shelby and I were still laughing as we headed for the doors.

"So much for being popular in junior high," I told Shelby when we got into the hall.

"Oh, well," Shelby smiled and said, "there's always high school.

"I gotta get to French," Shelby said as she looked at her class schedule. "Or should we protest classes, too?"

5

The rest of that week was pretty much the same routine. The only time I saw Shelby was at lunch, and we acted as silly as we had on the first day. The only difference was that we insisted on carrying brown paper bag lunches.

The same group of kids sat with us, and for a while, they seemed to have gotten used to me sitting there. But no one ever talked to either one of us. Occasionally a few of the kids peeked in our direction, but that was about it.

It must have been around the third week of school that everything changed. I was sitting by myself at the end of "our" table, enjoying a delicious sandwich that I'd loaded with cream cheese and cinnamon, when this tall blonde girl who usually sat at the far end of our table came and sat next to me. She placed her lunch tray on the table and began eating.

As usual, Shelby was late. Shelby and I always

sat in the same seats. I knew this girl realized that she was taking Shelby's seat.

I politely reminded her. "That's my friend's seat. She should be here in a second." The tall girl ignored me and went on eating her cafeteria food.

"Excuse me." I raised my voice a bit. "I said my friend is sitting there, it's okay if you want to sit there until she gets here — but then you'll have to move. . . ." The girl never looked at me, but she did jab me with a bony elbow.

"Hey! I don't want any trouble!" I stared at her hard. The girl smirked and looked away.

"Suit yourself." I elbowed her back. "Be rude and childish." I collected my lunch and got up from the table just as Shelby walked up.

Shelby opened her mouth to say something, but I grabbed her sweater, and steered her toward another table. The rude blonde girl called after Shelby, "You can sit here, but just don't bring *her* back!"

"What's going on?" Shelby looked back at the girl. "Who was she?"

"I don't know." I told Shelby all that had happened before she walked in.

"These people *are* rude," Shelby said, shaking her head.

"They just don't want me to sit at their table with them," I told Shelby. "I'm pretty sure it's because I'm black."

"I can't believe that, Amber."

"It's true."

"But it doesn't make any sense!" Shelby kept bumping into people on our way to search for a new table. "That stuff doesn't happen here — this is Brookeville. Where did they grow up?"

"I don't know, Shelby. But everything I said is true."

I could tell Shelby wasn't convinced at all. She didn't believe me. I didn't expect her to, either.

We found seats at the end of a table near the middle of the cafeteria, close to where all the black kids seemed to be sitting. Maybe we would be safer here. This was crazy — having to worry about where to sit in the cafeteria.

I didn't notice who was sitting at the other end of our new table until I sat down. It was a group of kids who I had never seen before, except for one girl — the girl who'd smiled at me in the bathroom. There were two boys on her right, and another girl on her left. I didn't mean to stare, but I was so fascinated by her fancy clothes. I was so envious of her style. But she caught my eye and smiled.

"Hi," she called to me. "Want to join us?" She motioned for me to scoot down to her end of the table. I looked at Shelby and she smiled. We began to gather our stuff and move.

"Thanks," I sort of whispered to the girl from the bathroom.

"Uh," I felt obligated to introduce us, "I'm Amber." I nodded at Shelby, who had launched into her bologna sandwich, and added, "This is my best friend, Shelby."

"I'm Tamara." The girl from the bathroom nodded to both of us and said, "This is Carolyn, Jake, and Mark." She looked at each kid as she introduced them.

"Hey," answered Carolyn.

"What's up?" Jake asked with a smile.

Mark sort of nodded, then continued to hum some song he had been humming for Jake ever since we had sat down.

"What school did you come from?" asked Tamara.

"Deer Run Park Elementary," Shelby answered before I could. Shelby loved to talk and to meet new people, which was fine with me, because it wasn't something I was very good at. At least that's what I thought.

"What about you guys?" Shelby asked.

"Glen View Elementary," Tamara answered. She looked back and forth from Shelby to me, then added, "We take buses here."

"Wow," Shelby looked at Tamara, "Glen View's a long way from here."

"Sure is," Carolyn piped in. "It's a forty-minute bus ride!"

31

"On a stinky bus!" interjected Jake. We all laughed at him. I looked across the table at Shelby, and she smiled at me. At least there were some friendly people here — at least there seemed to be.

6

"Ma, is Brookeville a prejudiced town?" I was in our dining room helping her polish the silverware. I was still thinking about the incident in the cafeteria earlier that day.

Ma looked up from the bowl she was cleaning and raised her eyebrows. She always raises her eyebrows when I say or ask something that she doesn't expect me to know anything about. She's got amber-colored eyes, like mine, and they get tiny and squinchy when I ask a difficult question. Her eyes were definitely getting squinchy.

"Prejudiced?" Ma asked, smiling her nervous smile. Ma always tries to smile, no matter how bad a situation gets. "Why would you ask something like that?" She looked back down at the bowl of cleaning solution.

"I don't know." I shrugged my shoulders and watched her swish the dirty cleaning rag around the bowl filled with the smelly mixture. "I was wondering how the grown-ups in Brookeville feel about people like us living here."

It was an embarrassing thing for me to ask. It made me just as uncomfortable to talk about it as it seemed to be for her to hear it. But I needed to know.

I'd heard stories about how she and Daddy had grown up in Georgia during the early sixties, when things were pretty bad between blacks and whites. Things were especially bad in the South: Blacks were not given the chance to get jobs and were not allowed to eat in certain restaurants back then. I know a lot about this because of social studies classes back at Deer Run Park Elementary. Ma and Daddy never really talked about those days, though I know they must have had some of those experiences. I also know that my grandparents were mad at my parents for choosing to bring Alexandra and me up in a suburb like Brookeville, where there were just a few black families.

"I don't know," I repeated. Ma still hadn't answered me.

She looked at me and said, "Brookeville is a *good* town. Good people — the best schools — and opportunities for you and your sister. You should be happy to be able to grow up in such a nice neighborhood."

"I *am* happy Ma," I reassured her. "I was just wondering." I was afraid to tell her about what happened earlier that day at school. I wanted to tell her how different the junior high was from my old elementary. The kids at Brookeville were different. They had different ideas of what was right and what was wrong. I know she would have been shocked to know how the white and black kids rarely sat together, and how one girl had told Shelby not to let me sit at their table anymore. I wanted to tell her everything, but I really didn't want her to worry. I wanted her to think that everything was fine.

Ma wanted everything to be perfect. She wanted all of us to be happy. She hated to hear about Daddy having a bad day at work, or that Alexandra was upset because she'd broken up with her boyfriend. She would especially hate to hear that I was having problems at school because I was black, and that my schoolmates thought it was wrong for Shelby and me to be best friends.

Luckily, the phone rang, breaking the uncomfortable silence between us. It was Shelby.

"Hey, Shel," I said, relieved to escape the weird conversation with Ma.

"Hey, Amber." I heard Shelby's familiar, bubbly voice, and immediately felt better. "What's up?"

"Wanna come over?" I asked. "We'll plan our birthday."

"Be right over," Shelby promised.

*   *   *

"Do you think they'll let us go?" Shelby asked after we'd settled down in my room, our favorite "plotting and planning" place. This time we were "plotting and planning" our thirteenth birthday celebration.

Shelby was worried that our parents would ruin our big plans. We were going all out this year.

I was worried, too.

We had planned this birthday back in the third grade. It had been fun dreaming about it all these years, but now it was exactly two months away, and we had to get moving.

"Amber, you're lucky 'cause your mom and dad are cool. They'll let you go. But my dad's gonna hit the roof, and Mom will say 'You're outta your mind!' " Shelby whined. Despite our worries, we couldn't help but laugh at Shelby's realistic impersonation of her mom.

This was the plan: Our birthdays were exactly eleven days apart. Mine was November ninth, and Shelby's was November twentieth. This year we had planned to celebrate on *my* birthday because it fell on a Saturday. This year, we were going to New York City — alone!

We would spend the day in Manhattan, then come home and prepare a big elegant dinner, in our honor, of course. All we had to do was to get our parents to agree to the best part — the New York City part.

36

I thought for a moment. We had to work this out somehow. "It's our thirteenth birthday," I reasoned, "they have to let us go. It will be our first year as *teen*-agers. We won't ask for any presents, just round-trip train tickets and permission to go."

"Great." Shelby gave me a doubtful smile. She was in her usual position, lying on my bed, staring at the ceiling.

"We're going!" I insisted. "Even if we have to sneak there."

Shelby sat up. "*Sneak* there?" she asked in disbelief. "Now you're outta *your* mind!"

"Nope. I'm just determined to have *the* best thirteenth birthday!" I told her.

"And I want to get a new outfit to wear to the city. A cool one, like the kids at school wear." I looked at Shelby. She had laid down again, eyes on the ceiling. And I knew that she was thinking about Patrick, once again. She claimed she was going through P.G.C.W. — Patrick *Gilbert* Connor Withdrawal — how stupid!

"Shelby." I was getting annoyed. "You're not paying attention. We have to get moving on our plans."

"I'm paying attention," Shelby insisted. "What have we got down in The Notebook so far?"

"The Notebook" was our special book that held all of our plans. We planned everything — birthdays, vacations, shopping sprees — and recorded it in this notebook. It was a simple gray spiral notebook, with *ANDERSON & ANDERSON* written on its cover, but it meant a lot to us. Our latest entry was all about our big thirteenth birthday plan. I read it aloud.

"We leave the house by 7:00 A.M., to make a 7:15 bus. The bus will take us to a train that'll take us into the city. We will spend the day in the city, shopping, sightseeing, and eating street food from vendors. We will return home by 7:00 P.M., in time to prepare our big dinner." I cleared my throat and grinned at Shelby.

"Anderson and Anderson eat and eat and eat," Shelby added. She held her two arms out to indicate a fat belly, then continued, "Until they almost burst!"

"No kidding!" I yelled in agreement.

"Well," I looked at Shelby for approval of our plans, "what do you think, Anderson?"

"Boy," Shelby smiled, "we should go into the birthday catering business. We've got everything down to a science."

"So what do you say, do we devise a plan and sneak to New York?" I *was* determined.

"How will we get away with being away from home for an entire day?" Shelby looked worried.

I pointed to my head, meaning I would think of something.

"We're going," I told her. "We'll worry about how, later."

I jumped on my bed in excitement. "I can't wait! I can't wait! I can't wait!" With each "I can't wait!" I jumped higher and higher on my bed, which also made Shelby bounce higher and higher. She tried to stand up and join my celebration, but my jumps kept making her lose her balance. She only managed to kneel and tried to pull me down with her. From her kneeling position, she joined my yells of, "I can't wait!"

This was going to be the best birthday ever. I was so excited that I forgot all about school and my talk with Ma. Those things didn't matter at this moment. Nothing was going to ruin my birthday.

I was sure of it.

7

After Shelby went home, I stretched out on my bed and watched the sky turn to a grayish-blue outside of my window. Sometimes when I am alone, and the house is quiet, I get this sad, lonely feeling while I watch the sky get ready for darkness. It's not a bad feeling. It's sorta relaxing. My sister, Alexandra, who is already a teenager, would probably call the feeling "romantic."

These are the times when I think about becoming a real teenager. I wonder if I'll always try to look perfect like Alexandra does, and constantly worry about my hair, makeup, and what the boys think of me.

Usually, I think about being twelve, and how much fun I've had this year. I worry that things will really change when I turn thirteen. Things were already beginning to change on my own body! I try to hide these changes from everyone else. My body might be ready for the changes, but I'm sure not ready for them. I'm scared.

This evening I thought about what was going on at school, and I really didn't understand why things were the way they were. I wasn't supposed to understand yet. Maybe it would become clearer when I turned thirteen, or sixteen, like Alexandra. Alexandra! She would understand. She could explain things to me. She didn't worry about being happy as much as Ma did. She realized that bad things went on in the world, too.

I had to pound on Alexandra's bedroom door four or five times before she heard me and opened it. She had her CD player turned all the way up.

"Hey, Alexandra, can I come in?" I yelled over the music. She widened her eyes, then smiled down at me. This was her way of telling me to come on in.

"Let me do your hair, Amber," Alexandra pleaded as she tugged at the end of my ponytail. "Let me try out a new hairstyle on you."

Hair, nails, clothes, boys! That was what my sister had turned into during the two years she had been attending Sherwood High. She had gone into the high school a shy, skinny kid like me — but with glasses. Two years later, she's this big-chested, curvy woman who all the guys try to speak to when she walks down the street. She had wanted to exchange her glasses for a pair of color-tinted contact lenses, but Daddy had a fit because she wanted blue ones.

"You weren't born with blue eyes, Alexandra,"

41

Daddy had told her. "You should be proud of what you have, and who you are — don't try to change."

Alexandra finally agreed to settle for plain, untinted contact lenses. She had to — Daddy was paying for them.

I was in Alexandra's room, preparing to bring up my question about the way the kids were acting at school. But as always, whenever I go into Alexandra's bedroom, I get distracted by all of the cool things in her room.

As soon as I walked in, I was immediately drawn to her CD collection — she must have at least a hundred! I pawed through the various discs, fascinated by the weird names of these bands and groups — The Rowdies, Popsickle, Mosaic Blues, and six discs by a goofy-looking guy called Mega-MC. Alexandra began her plea to transform me into a twelve-year-old beauty.

"Come on, Amber," she begged as she loosened my scrunchy ponytail holder. "Let's do your hair for your thirteenth birthday!"

"My birthday's not for another two months. You can do my hair then."

"But we'll practice now," she explained. "Besides, haven't you found a special guy at school who you want to surprise with a new look?"

"No," I answered honestly.

But poor Alexandra looked so disappointed that I finally gave in.

"Just don't put any goo in my hair," I warned her. She has dozens of jars, cans, and bottles filled with multicolored lotions and gels that she uses in her hair. She also relaxes her hair to tame the frizzy curls. I like my frizzy curls, and I didn't want any of Alexandra's hair goo to take them away.

As she brushed, combed, and parted my hair into various styles, I decided to talk to her about my problem.

"Alexandra," I hesitated, fearful of getting the same reaction from her as I had gotten from Ma. "Do you think Brookeville is a prejudiced town?"

Unlike Ma, she didn't seem at all surprised by my question.

"You can't label an entire town, Amber," she answered. "There are a lot of ignorant people in every town. Brookeville's no exception." She started to sigh. She does that when she says something she really believes is true. I knew I had come to the right person.

"I know," I answered, feeling grown-up having such an important conversation with my older sister. "But some towns are, on the whole, more prejudiced than others, right?"

She paused a second. I could tell she was getting her words together.

"Well," she finally answered, "I suppose towns that don't have many minorities will have more restrictions about the people they think belong in

43

the neighborhood than towns with more minorities."

I thought about that. I tried to put what she had said together, as she continued to brush my thick, tangled hair.

"I'm not sure what you mean," I replied. "Isn't that still wrong?" I tried really hard to sound just as mature as she did. Alexandra didn't get straight A's in school, but she was very smart.

"What I *mean*," Alexandra continued, emphasizing *mean*, "is that a town, like Brookeville, which does not have many minorities, might have some residents who feel a little funny about having minorities live near them, simply because they grew up without having the chance to meet different types of people, or to spend any time with them. And you're right, it is still wrong. It's their fault for not realizing that a person is a person, and that people will be good or bad no matter what color they are. But some people grow up believing one race is better than another. It's sad."

"But what about kids? Can they be ignorant, too?"

"Kids, too," Alexandra stated, then added, "they see how their parents treat certain people, and learn from them."

Wow. Alexandra did know what was going on. I wondered why Ma didn't answer me the way Alexandra had.

My new hairstyle turned out to be really cute.

44

Somehow, Alexandra had managed to tame my curly frizzies into a very sophisticated French twist. She left out wisps of bangs, and the whole look was great.

"I like it," I told Alexandra, as I examined my new look in her mirror. I would definitely let her do my hair for my birthday — for New York City!

I decided that I'd come visit Alexandra more often.

8

Usually, I hate Monday mornings. I get this icky feeling in my stomach starting Sunday night. My stomach feels like it's full of those imaginary butterflies. The icky feeling gets worse and worse, until I wake up on Monday morning. Then I'll realize why I'd been feeling this way. It's because I'm nervous about spending another week in junior high. I never used to get these feelings in elementary school. I read an article called "Do You Get the Monday Blues?" in this teen magazine last summer. That's what they called the icky feeling: The Monday Blues. The article did say it was normal to feel this way on Mondays, but if you feel this way every other day, too, then something could be wrong, and you should talk to a parent or school counselor. Luckily, it's only happened to me on Mondays, so far.

When I talked to Shelby on the phone the night before last, she and I had decided to wear our stretch pants with big, bulky sweatshirts and sneakers. I keep my sweatshirts folded in neat stacks on the shelves that cover one wall of my room. Most of my sweatshirts are collegiate gray or blue. Today I chose a pretty, sky-blue one.

It was October, and the weather was different every day. The week before it was so cold, I had to pull out my winter parka. But over the weekend it had gotten so warm that I had worn shorts.

I pressed my hand against my window to see if I could tell what the temperature was like. The window was cool, but not cold. My denim jacket would do.

"Amber, Alexandra, Phil!" Ma called. "Breakfast!" Her voice faded as she walked away from the bottom of the stairs and back into the kitchen.

She doesn't let *anyone* leave the house in the morning without eating breakfast. Usually, I have to force my food down because of my Monday Blues. But today I was starving. I could smell pancakes and sausage cooking, and I couldn't wait to eat.

Ma's a great Southern cook. Her mother, Grandma Pearl, was a famous cook. At least she was famous in Atlanta, where she grew up, and where she raised Ma, Uncle Chris, and Uncle Paul.

"I worked for white folks," Grandma Pearl would say. "The Emerson family in Atlanta. Big 'ol house made of stone. Biggest kitchen you'll e-e-e-ver see!"

Ma proudly tells the story of how the Emersons' dinner guests would enjoy Grandma Pearl's cooking so much, that they would beg Mr. Emerson to let them "buy Miss Pearl off," and come to work for them. But the Emersons always said, "No way," and they would get worried that they might lose Grandma Pearl, so they would give her a raise. She worked for them until Ma had Alexandra, then Grandma Pearl moved in with Ma and Daddy to help them with the new baby. She lived with our family until we moved from Queens. Now I only get to see her on holidays. I miss Grandma Pearl, but at least Ma learned all of her cooking talents from her. We lucked out!

"I didn't realize they were *blueberry* pancakes," I told Ma excitedly. She handed me the warm plate of soft, fluffy cakes with huge, round blueberries seeping out of them, covered with syrup.

"You don't eat enough, Amber," Ma complained. "You're as skinny as a little racehorse." Ma gets some of her expressions from Grandma Pearl, too.

"Well, I'm starving this morning, Ma," I told her as I dug my fork into the four layers of hotcakes, and added, "Just watch."

Shelby was standing by our lockers when I got to school. She looked cute in her pink sweatshirt and white stretch pants. She wore a pink scrunchy hairband that held her blonde ponytail on top of her head. She had the usual grin on her face.

"Hey, Amber!" Shelby squeezed my shoulder. She made me feel special when she greeted me like that — which was most of the time.

"Hey there, Shelby." I grinned back at her. I would give anything to be as bubbly and cute as my best friend. She always seemed to be having fun, no matter what.

"You look great," she said and shrugged her shoulders.

"You, too," I told her honestly, trying to sound just as bubbly as she did.

"Hurry and get your books," she said. "Let's go look at the Club Board."

"The Club Board?" I asked. What in the world was she talking about?

"Yeah, it's this big bulletin board that they put up by the gym, and all of the school clubs and organizations can post their sign-up sheets for new members. They're putting up the club lists for this year, today."

"Oh," I said, feeling stupid.

"*Shel*-by!" someone called from behind me.

Shelby widened her eyes to see who had called her. I turned to see, too. It was a tiny girl with really long, dark, straight hair.

"Hi, Shelby!" the girl belted out. She had a deep, husky voice. I almost laughed at how deep and loud it was, coming from such a little person. She walked up to Shelby.

"Oh, hi, Chloe." Shelby smiled — but it wasn't the same, fun greeting she had given me.

"Did you check out the Club Board yet?" she asked Shelby, in her deep voice.

"No, I, uh, we haven't looked yet." Shelby looked from Chloe to me. Then she said, "Uh, Chloe, this is my BEST friend, Amber Anderson. Amber, this is Chloe. Chloe's in three of my classes."

"Hi." I smiled with a stupid grin on my face and laughed my nervous laugh.

"Hi," answered the raspy-voiced Chloe. She glanced at me for only a second, then turned back to Shelby and said, "We'll have to get there soon, though. I hear that if they get too many people to sign up, they'll cut the lists, and give spaces to the first people who signed up. Let's go!"

Chloe grabbed Shelby's arm and pulled her along.

Shelby looked back at me and said, "Come on, Amber." I could tell she felt uncomfortable. I reluctantly followed the two of them down the hall. I felt so tall and awkward behind them, as if I didn't belong in their twosome. Shelby kept turning around to make sure I was following. I knew she would much rather be walking with just me. I was glad.

Chloe was kind of pushy and extremely talkative. And of course I didn't say a word. Shelby just grinned at her and listened to her talk and talk all the way to the gym.

"Shelby, who do you know?" Chloe asked. "Do you know Brad Daley or Mark Robson? They're *the* hottest guys in the seventh grade." Chloe was already popular at Brookeville Junior High, although she was only a seventh-grader. Every few steps we walked, a different kid would call out "Hi, Chloe!" to her.

When we got to the Club Board, there was already a crowd of kids there talking about the different clubs and signing their names on the lists. Chloe ran up to look at the lists. Shelby and I followed her.

"Check it out!" she belted out. "Spaces left to sign up for drill team and *cheerleading*." Chloe looked directly at Shelby when she said "cheerleading." Chloe had little freckles across her nose. Her nose was tiny, even tinier than Shelby's. I also noticed that she had green eyes. She was very pretty.

"The drill team's pretty nerdy, though," Chloe warned. "We'd better stick to cheerleading. Guys are hot for cheerleaders." She talked only to Shelby. She completely ignored me — not that I really cared.

"Gotta pen?" she asked Shelby.

"I think so," Shelby answered, as she filed through her book bag. She handed Chloe a pen

51

Chloe wrote her name on the list with the big *CHEERLEADING* written across the top. She had fancy handwriting. Her last name was Mora.

"Your turn, Shelby." She directed Shelby and handed her the pen. She actually meant for Shelby to sign up for cheerleading! I couldn't imagine Shelby as a cheerleader. Maybe in high school, but not now, not in junior high! I didn't want to try out for cheerleading now, and surely Shelby wouldn't want to try out without me. We did everything together.

"I haven't thought much about it, Chloe," Shelby admitted. She shrugged her shoulders and smiled at Chloe. "I don't think I'd make a good cheerleader, anyway."

Chloe turned around to face Shelby and said, "*Shel*-by, you gotta try out for cheerleading. You'll be great. You want to be popular, don't you?" She whispered this last part into Shelby's ear. But her husky voice carried to my ears, too.

"Well." Shelby looked up at the list Chloe had written her name on, then looked at me.

"Amber, you too?" Shelby asked.

Until then, I felt I had nothing to say in the matter. But now, Shelby was putting me on the spot.

"I don't know, Shel." I tried to whisper so only she would hear, but Chloe looked me right in the eyes and heard everything.

"Come on, Shelby," Chloe begged, completely ignoring what I had just said.

"Only if Amber does." Shelby stated this firmly. Good old Shelby! Chloe rolled her eyes and stared back up at the Club Board. Shelby was my buddy. We've always stuck together. This time wouldn't be any different. At least that's what I thought.

Shelby sighed. "Well, I don't know," she hesitated. "Maybe."

"Maybe?" Chloe asked.

Maybe? I asked too, but not out loud.

I couldn't believe what I'd just heard. She was actually considering doing something I didn't want to do.

"I don't think *I* will," I told Shelby, purposely looking away from Chloe. Then I surprised myself by adding, "But you go ahead, Shel, if you really want to." I said it, but I didn't mean it. But I knew Shelby. I saw that she really did want to try this. Who wouldn't? Like Chloe had said, cheerleaders were the most popular girls in school. But I didn't belong in cheerleading. Cheerleaders were bubbly and cute like Chloe and Shelby. I was too awkward and skinny. It just wasn't me.

"Besides," I tried to sound like it didn't bother me at all, "I'd rather do something like — join the chorus!"

As soon as I said this, I saw Chloe push her lips together hard. She was trying not to laugh.

She was going to ruin everything. I wanted to tell her to shut up so badly, but I didn't.

I giggled nervously for no reason. I felt so out of place, and so embarrassed.

Shelby began to shake her head "no," but I reached out and squeezed her shoulder like she had done to me earlier — before Chloe had arrived.

"It's okay," I mouthed to her.

Shelby smiled at me, then looked back up at the list.

"Come on!" Chloe nudged Shelby.

"Amber, are you sure you won't sign up with us?" Shelby pleaded. "It'll be so much fun. If we make it, we'll wear uniforms and everything."

"No, you go ahead. Honestly." I kept nodding my head.

Shelby looked down at her shoes and said, "I don't know why I'm signing up, either. I know I won't make it. But I'll try." She wrote her name on the list. Chloe grinned with approval.

"I know I won't make it," Shelby said again. "They want fun, peppy girls. Probably ones who can do cartwheels, too. I can't do cartwheels."

"I'll teach you," Chloe promised her. "It's easy. I cheered for Silver Springs Elementary last year. I'll help you, Shelby."

When Shelby finished signing her name, she looked at me again. She was making sure it was okay with me. I forced myself to smile again. And again, I nodded my head.

Chloe went on and on about how she and Shelby could get together before tryouts and practice, and how she just *knew* they would both make it, and have so much fun at the games, and how all the hot guys would want to meet them.

She just wouldn't shut up!

Finally, I couldn't take it anymore, so I turned to Shelby and said, "Shel, I have to run to Spanish. Ms. Egell hinted that she might give us a pop quiz this morning. I want to get some studying done before class."

Shelby hesitated, then said, "Sure, see you later, Amber. At lunch?" She gave me a worried look.

"Of course," I reassured her.

"Same table?" she asked.

"Same table. See you then." I walked away as fast as I could. As I left, I heard Chloe say to Shelby, "I thought *we'd* sit together at lunch, and figure out when we would practice for cheerleading."

I didn't hear Shelby's answer.

9

Shelby must have said no to Chloe's lunch offer, because when I got to the cafeteria door, Shelby was waiting for me.

"Hi, Amber." She had a funny smile on her face. She was worried about something. Probably the cheerleading thing.

All through Spanish class I had thought about Shelby and this cheerleading idea. Shelby had never told me she had any interest in cheerleading. I always teased her about being the cheerleading type — when we got to high school. But I never believed she would actually go through with it in junior high!

I was feeling weird about Chloe, too. I couldn't help but feel jealous. Back at Deer Run Park, Shelby and I had always been a twosome. Sure, we had other friends like Sherry Sutherland and Jamie Mitchell. All four of us would meet at the mall on Saturdays, or go to the movies on Sunday afternoons. But everything else only included me and Shelby. Except for the time Shelby couldn't come with me to camp, she and I have always done the important things together, like visiting my grandma in Georgia, or joining our favorite band's fan club. But trying out for cheerleading was something we had never talked about before.

"Hi, Shelby."

"Let's go to our table." She began to walk toward the table where Tamara and her friends sometimes sat. Today they weren't at the table. Sometimes they would spend lunch hour in the bathrooms. "We can be ourselves in there," they claimed. "How's that?" Shelby had asked them once. "Black," they'd replied.

After we had unpacked our brown bag lunches, and compared our food, and traded this for that, and giggled at the runny tuna sandwich her mother had packed, Shelby turned to me and said, "I really don't want to try out for cheerleading without you, Amber. It wouldn't be fun."

I didn't look at her. I got a lump in my throat. I felt like crying for no reason, so I played it safe and just didn't say anything.

"Honestly, Amber, please tell me if you don't want me to go through with it. It's no big deal to me."

"But boy, would Chloe be disappointed," I said a little too sarcastically.

"Oh, Amber, stop! I knew you would think I was doing it because of her! And it's not true."

She took a bite of her sandwich and said with a full mouth, "I've always wondered what it would be like to be a cheerleader. They're so popular and fun. And they always look like they're having the greatest time. Anyway, I know I won't make it."

She wanted me to say, "Yes you will, Shelby." But I didn't. Instead, I just shrugged my shoulders and said, "I don't care." But I really did care — a lot.

"Amber?" Shelby looked at me again. This time I looked back at her.

"I really won't do it if you don't want — "

"Do it," I told her, "you've got a good chance. You are fun! I know you would make a great cheerleader."

"But do it with me?" she pleaded.

"No," I answered, "I really don't want to."

"Well, thanks for telling me you don't mind if I do."

"It's okay," I lied.

10

Shelby and I didn't have lunch together the next day, or the day after that. As a matter of fact, we didn't have lunch together for the rest of the week. The Club Board had posted a notice that *ALL PROSPECTIVE CHEERLEADERS* had to meet every day from 3:30 until 4:00 to learn the cheers that would be used at the tryouts. Each prospective cheerleader was to be paired with another prospective cheerleader, and the two of them would perform one cheer that was taught to them, and one that they made up themselves. They would perform in front of the judges on Friday.

Chloe insisted that she and Shelby be partners and, in order for them to be prepared, they would have to practice every day during lunch

Since we didn't have any classes together, I didn't get to see her during the day. After school, she had to practice in the gym with the other girls who were going to try out. Every morning we met at our lockers and she would promise to come over to my house after practice. Every evening she would call to apologize, and say she was so achy and tired and couldn't make it.

School was lonely enough without having Shelby in any of my classes, but school was even lonelier knowing I wouldn't see her at lunch or after school.

One day during lunch I sat with Tamara and her friends. They tried to include me in their conversations, but I still felt so out of place. They had all known each other from their elementary school, and talked about kids and places that I didn't know.

"Amber, where do you live?" Sheila, one of Tamara's friends asked me.

"Here in Brookeville," I answered. "Only four blocks away from school."

Sheila gave Tamara, and their other friend, Pam, a funny look. Both Tamara and Pam smirked.

"I thought Brookeville was all white," Tamara responded.

"What do you mean by 'all white'?" I asked. I had a pretty good idea of what she meant.

"I mean, all white people live here," she answered. Her friends still had funny looks on their faces. Tamara just looked really serious.

"No," I said quickly. "Of course not. There are at least three other black families besides mine in the neighborhood. There aren't very many, but it's *not* 'all white.' "

"Have you lived here all of your life?" Pam asked me.

"No. I was born in Queens, and lived there until I was eight."

"I have folks in Queens — Astoria," Sheila told me.

"Really?" was all I could think of to say. They were making me feel very self-conscious.

That's all I said for a while, until, out of the blue, Sheila asked me, "So, Amber, where's that white girl you usually eat with?"

I didn't like the way she had said that *white girl*. She had been introduced to Shelby, and knew her name. I was offended.

"My best friend, Shelby?" I asked, putting an emphasis on *best*. "She's trying out for cheerleading, and she's been busy practicing this week."

"Man, they should get some real cheerleaders at this school," Sheila said. "They need to get their act together."

"I know," Pam agreed. "They need some *sisters* on the squad."

"They'd never do that. They'd never put a SISTER on the squad here!" Tamara yelled.

"You know it!" Sheila and Pam both roared.

They really didn't think Brookeville Junior High would allow any black girls on the squad? That would be discrimination!

"Why do you say that?" I asked them. "How do you know there won't be any black girls on the squad? I know there's at least four trying out."

"Yeah, let's see if they make it," Joyce said, then laughed. Tamara and Pam laughed, too.

"One will make it," Pam said. "She'll be their 'token.' " This made the three of them laugh even more. I smiled, so that they'd think I understood what they were talking about. I was really confused. Maybe they were right. I thought about what Alexandra had said about places where there aren't many minorities. There weren't many blacks at Brookeville Junior High. Tamara and her friends came all the way from Glen View. If they weren't here, there would be less than a dozen black kids in the whole school. But I still refused to believe that it was as bad as these girls thought it was.

"Were you guys cheerleaders at Glen View?" I asked.

"Tamara was," Sheila answered.

"She was a captain!" added Pam.

"You were?" I looked at Tamara, who was sitting back in her chair with her arms folded.

"Yep," she answered. "We had some bumpin' cheers, too!"

"You know it," said Sheila.

"Why don't you try out for Brookeville's squad?" I asked Tamara. "If you were a captain at Glen View, you'd have a great chance. My friend Shelby's never even been a cheerleader, and she's trying out. She doesn't even know how to do a cartwheel!"

"Yeah, right." Tamara rolled her eyes, and looked at her friends. "And let me be the *token*? No thank you."

I shrugged my shoulders and kept quiet for the rest of the lunch hour.

11

On Friday morning, Shelby wasn't at her locker. It's rare that we walk to school together because she has to walk her little sister, Paige, to school before she comes to Brookeville. Sometimes she's a little late and comes running in minutes before the first class bell. This morning, I figured she had come in earlier to practice in the gym with Chloe. When I spoke to her on the phone last night, she said Chloe wanted to meet early this morning.

Today was her big day — cheerleading tryouts. And she told me she was really nervous.

"You've gotta stay after with me, Amber," Shelby insisted over the phone. "I need you there for good luck."

"They probably won't let me in to watch."

"But you'll be there to wish me luck before I go in. And," she added, "you'll be there afterwards, when I come out crying because everyone laughed at me."

"No, I'll be there to help you celebrate your victory!"

"Does that mean you'll stay?" she asked hopefully.

"Sure," I gave in, "I'll be there."

Actually, I was kind of relieved that all of this cheerleading stuff would be over with after this afternoon. Most likely, Shelby wouldn't make the squad. She really didn't have the experience. That meant no more lunches without Shelby. No more boring afternoons. No more Chloe!

Just as I was about to close my locker and head for Spanish class, Shelby came running down the hall. The first thing I noticed was that she wasn't wearing purple, like we had promised each other last night.

"Hey," I waved to her as she ran up to me. "Where's your purple?" She was wearing a blue miniskirt and a gold sweater. She had pulled her hair into two ponytails. She looked like a real cheerleader!

"Chloe said we should wear the school colors to show our spirit." Shelby opened her locker and began rummaging through it, then continued, "She says the judges will be watching us all day."

"That's dumb," I said to her. "They'll only be watching you at the tryouts!" Chloe had all of these weird rules and ideas about cheerleading she had been making up all week. Shelby was included in all of them. I was tired of it.

"I really don't understand it myself," Shelby admitted. "But I figured Chloe knew better than I did."

"You're still waiting for me, aren't you?" Shelby asked as she looked at me. She was really worried.

"Of course," I promised again, "I'll be there."

Shelby smiled at me and said, "Great."

The last warning bell rang, and Shelby panicked. "Oh, no, I'm going to be late again. I haven't even read my social studies assignment that we're being quizzed on this morning! What the heck am I gonna do?"

I'd never seen Shelby get so frustrated. "Just relax, Shelby. Things will work out." I tried to calm her down.

Shelby took a deep breath. "Sorry," she sighed and tried to smile, but I could tell she was still upset. We both began fumbling with our locks.

"What's this?" Shelby picked up a small white envelope that had fallen out of her locker.

"Someone must have slipped this letter in my locker."

"Maybe it's something about cheerleading," I offered. "Look Shel, I'll see you later — probably not until after school, at your tryouts."

"Okay," Shelby answered. "Just be sure to show up."

I left her by the lockers, examining her mysterious white envelope. It wasn't until later that I found out what it was.

"Did you get your invitation, Amber?" Shelby surprised me by showing up at the cafeteria door after lunch.

"Did I get my invitation to what?"

"Maryanne's party," she said, as if I should have known this all along.

"Whose party? What invitation?" I asked, baffled.

"Maryanne Sarano's giving a big Halloween party. She invited the whole seventh grade, and a few eighth-graders. Boys, too." Shelby whispered this last part to me and grinned.

"Maybe even P.C.," she added.

"Who's P.C.?" I asked.

"You know, Patrick Connor." She looked at me as if I was intentionally being stupid about everything. I didn't know anything about the party. I didn't even know who Maryanne Sarano was. And I'd *never* heard Shelby refer to Patrick Connor as P.C.

"Oh," Shelby covered her mouth, and sort of snickered, "that was Chloe who suggested I call him P.C."

"You told Chloe about Patrick?" I asked, shocked. I thought that was our secret.

"Just a little," Shelby said quietly. "I just told her I thought he was cute."

I shrugged my shoulders and pretended not to mind. Shelby had barely mentioned him lately. She must have saved it all for Chloe.

"And what were you saying about a party?" I asked, partly to change the subject, and partly because I was curious to know how Shelby knew about the party and I didn't. Suddenly, I felt like I'd missed out on a lot of what was going on in Shelby's life. I used to be the first one to know what was going on with her, and now it seemed like I was always the last.

"Well," Shelby paused for a second, "Maryanne Sarano is a girl in Chloe's and my English class. I don't really know her, but she passed out invitations early this morning to her Halloween party. She got a list of all the seventh-graders' locker numbers from the office. That's what was in that white envelope I found in my locker this morning."

"Oh," I said, nodding my head. I began walking toward my English class. Shelby followed.

"I didn't get an invitation, Shelby," I told her.

"Sure you did. You must have. All the seventh-graders did," she insisted. "Even people Maryanne doesn't know too well got one."

"Shelby, I'm sure I didn't."

"It must still be in your locker. Check for it later."

"Okay," I answered, doubtful. I kept tons of junk in my locker. It was possible that I could have overlooked it. Maybe it had gotten stuck in between some books or something.

"I'll look later," I agreed.

She smiled before she turned to head in the direction of her next class. " 'Bye, Amber. Don't forget about tryouts!"

"I won't," I promised.

12

I didn't get an invitation.

Right after my last class, I ran to my locker just to look for it. Shelby had pretty much convinced me that it would be there. Surely, if Shelby had been invited, and she didn't know this Maryanne girl, either, I would be invited. Everyone knew that Shelby and I were best friends.

But when I searched my locker, I didn't find anything. I even shook out all of my books to make sure it hadn't gotten caught in between the pages. There was no white envelope in my locker.

Maybe there had been a mistake. There had to be a reason why I wasn't invited to the big party. By the end of the day, I had heard all about Maryanne Sarano's party. All the kids were talking about it. I even heard about it from Maryanne herself, but she didn't say anything directly to me. On the way to my last period class, this blond guy ran up to a really tall girl with brown hair and

70

said, "Thanks for inviting me to the bash, Mary-anne. I heard everyone's going to be there."

"Yeah," said Maryanne, turning to look down on the blond guy, who was at least a foot shorter than she was. "I invited all the seventh-graders. I figured the party would be a good way to really start getting to know each other. After all, we're all stuck here for two more years!"

Even as I stood by my locker that afternoon, about a dozen other kids opened their lockers to discover a white envelope like Shelby had gotten.

"Did you get invited?" everyone was asking each other.

"Of course," other kids would answer, "every-one did!"

Everyone did not. I didn't.

Oh, well, I thought, I can't worry about that now. I had to get to the gym to make sure I saw Shelby before her cheerleading tryouts. I wanted to wish her luck. I would also ask her about the party, and tell her that I didn't get an invitation. She was in one of Maryanne's classes. Maybe she could mention to Maryanne that she had over-looked my locker. I walked quickly to the gym.

Shelby's big tryouts were finally happening. I wondered if she had a chance at all. People like Chloe had been cheerleaders at their elementary schools. And Shelby couldn't even do a cartwheel. I made myself hope that she would make it. It was hard to hope for something like that, because deep down inside, I knew I *didn't* really want it to happen.

When I got to the gym, there were at least fifty other kids waiting outside. They were all trying to watch the tryouts through the glass windows of the gym doors.

Ms. West, the gym teacher, came to the door to quiet us down.

"Sh-h-h." She held her finger in front of her mouth. "You kids have to keep quiet, or else I'll have to ask you to leave the building."

I'd hoped to get to the gym before Shelby went in. I really wanted her to know that I was there.

"Good luck, Marcie!" someone yelled.

"Break a leg or two, Janet!" someone else screamed.

I even heard a "Way to go, Chloe!"

Good luck, Shelby, I said to myself.

I didn't even try to get to the doors of the gym, there were so many kids in the way. Soon we heard the school song blast over the gym stereo system.

Da, da, da, da-a-a-a! A horn sounded.

Even though I had only been at Brookeville Junior High for two months, I figured I had heard that school song so many times, I could sing it by heart.

"What's going on in there?" asked a girl who stood near me.

"They're all just marching around, carrying pom-poms," answered a tall guy who could see through the windows. "Now they're just standing there."

"Sh-h-h," someone else said. "Listen." We all leaned closer to the doors.

"READY, O-K!" yelled two girls.
"SHOUT IT FROM THE EAST,
SHOUT IT FROM THE WEST,
WE'RE THE TEAM FROM BROOKEVILLE
AND
WE KNOW THAT WE'RE
THE BEST!"

After the first two girls had recited the cheer at the top of their lungs, they did a couple of jumps and went into a cheer they'd made up themselves.

The Brookeville cheer was repeated over and over by eight other girls, before I heard something that woke me from my daze.

"Next up, Mora and Anderson!" Ms. West bellowed. "Please take your places!"

It was Shelby's turn! I elbowed my way through the crowd to try to get closer to the door. I still couldn't see anything, but I could hear them. They sounded great!

I heard Chloe's eager, raspy voice, and Shelby was keeping right up with her. I had never heard

Shelby yell so loudly in all the years I had known her.

"WE KNOW THAT WE'RE . . . THE BEST!" they cheered. But Shelby and Chloe had come up with a surprise ending:

"THE BEST (hey, hey), THE BEST (hey, yeah)," they added while fading their voices out.

"Whoa-o--o!" cheered all the kids outside of the gym. Even a few of their competitors cheered for them, too. They were definitely the best so far!

But then, what was even more surprising, was the cheer they had made up themselves. It went something like this:

"HEY, SHELBY!"
"HEY, CHLOE!"
"WHO'S THE HOTTEST TEAM 'YA
    KNOW?!"
"THEY CALL THEMSELVES THE
    BROOKEVILLE BEARS!
THEY'RE HOT! THEY'RE HOT!
THEY GIVE 'EM ALL THEY'VE GOT!"

"They were great!" someone yelled when Shelby and Chloe had finished.

"Of *course* Chloe will make it," a red-haired girl with glasses said to the girl beside her.

Finally, after what seemed like hours, we heard Ms. West call out, "Parker and Beuchler — the last girls!" They were awful. One of them forgot the cheer, and the other one found this so funny that all she did was laugh. The kids out in the hall, including me, laughed, too. Finally, Ms. West yelled, "That's enough, girls, thank you!"

By that time, I was so tired that I sat down on the floor. Inside the gym, Ms. West went on and on about how there was only room for ten cheerleaders, and two co-captains. She told them they had all tried their best, and should be proud. She ended by telling them to go home and soak their feet, and the results would be posted on the Club Board, Monday morning.

Suddenly, the doors burst open, and the mob of "prospective cheerleaders" rushed out of the gym. Shelby was the second girl out, with Chloe only inches behind her. She ran up to me.

"Did you see me, Amber, did you get to see me?" Her face was red with excitement.

"They wouldn't let us in," I told her. "But I heard you, and you sounded great!" I said honestly.

Shelby looked over at Chloe, who had been talking to some of her friends, then said, "I owe it all to Chloe. She taught me everything. You should have seen me on Monday. I was a disaster!" She looked at Chloe again, and the two of them burst into hysterics. I smiled politely, and looked at both of them. I felt like I didn't belong there. I felt left out.

"Aw, Shelby," Chloe blurted out between giggles, "you weren't *that* bad."

"Oh, yes I was," Shelby insisted. "You pushed me until I got better. You were a great coach."

"Well, we're not on the squad yet," Chloe reminded Shelby. She put her arm around Shelby's shoulder, the way I used to, and said, "But we're a shoo-in team."

"That's great," I said softly, with a phony smile still pasted on my face. I didn't know what else to say or do.

"It sure helped that we worked as a team," Shelby replied, putting her arm around Chloe's shoulder. She and Chloe were the exact same height.

"Mora and Anderson," Chloe held out her free hand for Shelby to slap.

Shelby slapped Chloe's hand with her free hand, and repeated, "Mora and Anderson," but she looked sideways at me right after she said it, and winked. Nothing could beat "Anderson and Anderson," even if the two of them made the cheerleading squad.

Just then, another group of girls who'd also tried out for the squad ran up to Chloe and told her how good she was. They turned to Shelby, too, and told her she'd done a great job. Shelby thanked them, and re-told the story of how awful she was at the beginning of the week, and how she "owed it all" to Chloe.

Shelby stood out in their group. They all wore

a ton of eyeshadow and blush and had too much goo in their hair. Shelby's clean skin and naturally curly blonde hair didn't fit in. I backed away from them and moved against the wall. I realized that I stood out even more than Shelby.

Shelby noticed I had moved away and came over to me. "Amber, I'm actually free this afternoon. Come over to my house, and we'll create."

"Create" was Shelby and my way of saying we'll make a mess of the kitchen by trying out a new recipe. Some of them have been very creative. They're rarely edible, but it's fun to try.

"You can sleep over, too," she added.

"Sure," I said. It would be great having Shelby to myself again.

Chloe came over to where we were standing, and jabbed Shelby in the arm.

"Hey, Bonehead," she said jokingly to Shelby. "The group's going to hang out at the mall. Wanna come?"

"No thanks, Chloe." Shelby shook her head. "Amber and I have plans."

I was glad Shelby had said we had plans, instead of telling her about our cooking, and me sleeping over. "Plans" sounded more mysterious and grown-up.

"I thought you would want to spend some time with the group, Shelby," Chloe said.

"No, thanks," Shelby answered without hesitation.

Chloe looked at me as if she had noticed me for the first time ever. She had never spoken directly to me, except for last Monday, when Shelby first introduced us, and she'd said hi. But then again, I had never said anything to her, either. Whenever I saw her in the halls, I tried to catch her eye and say hello, just to be polite. But she never looked my way.

"Have fun then," she said with a shrug. She kept looking at me so I answered, "Thanks, you too."

She turned back to Shelby and said, "Oh yeah, we still have a date tomorrow to make our costumes, don't we? Maryanne's Halloween party will be here before we know it."

"O-o-o, I forgot," Shelby bit her lip, then turned to me and explained, "Chloe and I were going to be something cute, like cats, for Maryanne's party, and wear leotards and stockings, and make tails and ears."

"P.C. will *love* you in that!" Chloe yelled.

"P.C.'s going, Amber. Maryanne invited him," Shelby told me. "Can you believe it? Amber, you can be a cat, too. We could be the three little kittens. Amber, too?" She turned to Chloe.

Chloe gave me a funny look and didn't say anything, so I spoke up. "Shelby, I wasn't invited to the party."

Shelby looked at me with a confused expression.

"Sure you were. Check for the invitation in your locker."

"I did," I told her. I started to get a lump in my throat. This was beginning to be a regular thing these days. "There . . . was no . . . invitation."

"You must have been invited. Maryanne invited everyone, right, Chloe?"

Chloe raised her eyebrows and answered, "Well, I doubt she invited any — " she hesitated, "Well, you know." She smiled nervously, and looked at Shelby, then me.

"What are you talking about?" Shelby asked Chloe.

Chloe resumed her usual "cool" expression. "I don't know, she probably doesn't know . . . Amber."

"Well, we'll have to talk to her then," Shelby rolled her eyes. "She must have made a mistake. There are so many seventh-graders. We'll talk to her, Amber. We'll make sure you get invited, right, Chloe?"

Chloe didn't say anything.

13

"Phe-e-ew!" Shelby let out a long, whistling breath when we got outside. "What a long, hard week. I'm so behind in my homework, I'll never catch up."

"Well, you know, Shel, if you get on the squad, it'll take up just as much time."

"I know. That's why I don't know if I'm ready for all of this. I'm sure it would be fun and all, but — I'm not nearly as good as Chloe and the other girls. I'll look like a klutz compared to them."

"Don't worry so much," I told her.

We didn't say much of anything else as we walked to her house. I knew she was thinking about being on the squad. And while Shelby thought about herself, I suddenly found myself thinking about me.

Me. That's something I hadn't thought about in a while. I realized I had never signed up for chorus, and wondered if it was too late. There hadn't been too many names on the Club Board list. I would have to find out.

Before we got up the stairs to Shelby's house, her little sister, Paige, threw open the door to greet us.

"Shelby's home! Shelby's home!" she yelled and jumped up and down. "And Amber, too!" she added.

Paige loves Shelby and me. She calls us the "big girls" and always wants to do everything we do.

"Mommy, I wanna go to the mall with the big girls," she'd say. She's really sweet. She looks like a miniature Shelby.

"Hi, Paige." Shelby pulled at the curls in Paige's long blonde ponytail. Paige was wearing all pink and looked like a little bunny.

"Hi, Paige." I patted her little head. When we were inside, she followed us wherever we went.

"What are you big girls going to do tonight?" she asked. "Can I play, too?"

"We'll see," Shelby told her.

Shelby's mom came out of her studio. She's a fashion designer and makes a lot of neat things. Shelby and Chloe would probably ask her to help them with their costumes.

"Hi, Honey Bun." She kissed Shelby. Mrs. Anderson has curly blonde hair like Shelby and Paige. She's skinny on top, but has a wide bottom.

"Amber Anderson!" Mrs. Anderson gave me a big hug. "I haven't seen you in years," she exaggerated.

I laughed and said, "I know, junior high is a lot busier than elementary school. And Shelby's been busy with cheerleading tryouts."

"That's right, today was the big day. Shelby, tell me all about the tryouts." She turned back to Shelby. "How did you and Chloe do?"

"We were fan-tas-tic!" Shelby blurted out. She told her mom all about the tryouts, and once again, gave Chloe all the credit.

"Honey Bun, it was *your* skill though," Mrs. Anderson said.

"Anyway, I won't make it," Shelby insisted.

"She'll make it," I told Mrs. Anderson. "She sounded great."

"Shelby's a cheerleader! Shelby's a cheerleader!" Paige danced around and sang.

"Not yet," Shelby corrected her.

Mrs. Anderson pinched Shelby's cheeks teasingly and said, "You'll make it."

Shelby rolled her eyes and smiled. "Mom, can we use the kitchen? We're going to be creative."

"Just clean up afterwards," Mrs. Anderson answered, "and let me have a taste of whatever you make." She winked at both of us.

"Me, too," Paige insisted. "Can I help, too?"

"I guess," Shelby told her.

We decided to make a peach cobbler. We used

canned peaches and stewed them with sugar and lemon juice. Paige turned out to be a hard worker, too. We all got silly while the cobbler baked.

Shelby switched on the radio to WWEX and we all started dancing around and singing at the top of our lungs. It felt like old times again.

14

Shelby's phone rang at 9:30 Saturday morning and jolted me out of a dream about — Patrick Connor! At first I thought I was in my own bed, and it confused me when I saw Shelby in the twin bed next to me. Shelby also jumped when the phone rang. She jumped all the way out of bed.

"Who the heck is calling at 9:30 on a Saturday morning?" she asked in a croaky frog voice. We had stayed up way past midnight watching a movie on video, then we talked for at least another hour about our birthday plans. Shelby reassured me we were still going through with them.

Shelby's dad must have answered the phone. About two minutes later we heard his deep voice yell from his and Mrs. Anderson's room, "Shelby! You up? The phone's for you!"

"Okay, Daddy!" Shelby attempted to call back. She still had the frog. She cleared her throat, then walked into the hall to get the phone.

Shelby doesn't have a phone in her room. Mrs.

84

Anderson says it's because Shelby would be tempted to stay on it all day and all night, talking to me, and never get her homework done. Mrs. Anderson's probably right.

I wondered who was calling Shelby so early. Maybe it was Patrick. The way things were going lately, I wouldn't be surprised if she were getting calls from boys and not telling me!

As I waited for Shelby to come back, I thought about the dream I'd had about Patrick. It was weird. In the dream, he was standing in the hall at school, signing autographs! When it was my turn to get his autograph, he said, "Amber Anderson, I didn't know *you* liked me, too." He was so cute that I blushed. The bell rang for class, and I told him I had to run, or I would be late. That was when I realized it wasn't the class bell ringing after all. It was Shelby's telephone.

Shelby sure was having a long conversation. I got out of bed and stretched. I looked around Shelby's room. She had the same wallpaper on the walls, and the same comforters on the twin beds that she's had since I've known her. The walls are covered with tiny pink ballet slippers, and her comforters are made of frilly-soft pink organdy.

I had just pulled off my pajama top, when Shelby came back. She stared at my chest and exclaimed, "Wow, you're growing! You'll have to start wearing a bra all the time like me."

"Oh, no," I quickly shook my head. "Not until it's absolutely necessary. I feel like I'm wearing a harness when I'm wearing one of those." I quickly pulled on my T-shirt.

Shelby went to her closet and began searching for clothes to put on.

"Who was on the phone?" I asked her, trying not to sound too nosy. I was curious why she hadn't mentioned the call as soon as she came back to the room.

"It was — just Chloe," she answered. She lowered her voice when she said Chloe.

She didn't say anything else, so I asked, "About making costumes today?"

She nodded. She pulled a shirt from a hanger in the closet and didn't look at me at all. I knew something was wrong.

"Look, Shel." I sat on "my" twin bed. "I'll leave right now if you and Chloe need to get started . . ."

"Oh, Amber!" Shelby threw her shirt on the floor. "Chloe's so stupid!" She plopped down on the floor next to the shirt she had thrown down. "She says crazy things."

"What do you mean?" I asked her. She was really beginning to scare me.

"I was telling her how rude it was that Maryanne hadn't invited you to the party, and how it all must have been a mistake."

"And what did she say?" I asked.

Shelby shrugged without saying anything. She kept staring at her shirt.

Finally she said, "Chloe says crazy things all the time. She says dumb things. She *confuses* me."

I looked at Shelby. She wouldn't look at me.

"What does she say?" I asked again, quietly. I kept looking at her.

She opened her mouth to speak. At first, no sound would come out.

Finally she managed to say, "Things — about you." Her voice was shaky when she said "you."

Angrily, I hit the bed with my fist, and got up to put on the rest of my clothes. I didn't want to know what *Chloe* had said about me. But Shelby told me anyway.

"Chloe says I shouldn't hang around you all the time," she began. "She says none of the other kids will want to be my friend." Her voice was really shaking now.

I walked closer to where Shelby was sitting. "What — else — does — she say?" I demanded. My teeth were clenched, and my jaw was shaking when I said this. A big tear rolled out of Shelby's eye. Usually when I see Shelby cry, I immediately start crying, too, even if I don't feel sad. But this time I didn't. I was too mad.

"She says . . ." Shelby's voice was shaking. She swallowed, then continued, "Maryanne is not going to invite you to the party because — "

"Why?" I asked, even though I already had a good idea.

"Because she didn't invite anyone from Glen View. Maryanne thinks Glen View kids are no good."

"I'm not from Glen View!" I yelled in a deep, scary voice.

"*I* know that. I told Chloe that. But . . ."

"But it didn't matter," I finished her sentence for her. "Maryanne just didn't invite me because I'm BLACK!" I yelled to Shelby. I got really close to her. I was standing right over her. I felt like a mother. She looked like a really little girl, sitting on the floor, crying.

"*Right*, Shelby?" I asked in my deep, scary voice. "Am I right?"

She opened her mouth to say something, but before she could say anything I yelled, "I am leaving HERE! I don't want to be around people like *you*! You're just as bad, Shelby, you're just like all of them!" I couldn't believe I was saying these things to my best friend. She just looked at the floor and cried. She tried to say something, but I wouldn't let her.

"You go be with Chloe, and have a good time making fun of PEOPLE LIKE ME! You go be with her and her stupid, ignorant friends. You're worse than them, Shelby, because you only pretended to be my friend. But you really feel the same way they do!"

"NO!" Shelby yelled.

I couldn't stand it any longer. I had so many more bad things to say to her. But I was shaking too hard, and I felt like I was going to throw up. I grabbed my things and ran out of her room. I slammed the door really hard behind me. Shelby's parents came out of their room to see what was going on. I just ran past them and down the stairs.

As I ran out of the house, I could hear Shelby yelling, "I'm not like them, Amber! I'm not! Amber! AMBER!"

15

I wasn't speaking to Shelby — not after what had happened that morning. I wouldn't take her calls. Ma didn't understand, and I didn't feel like explaining.

"Don't be smart with me, young lady." Ma was serious.

"I'm not," I insisted.

"Then tell me this instant why you are avoiding Shelby's phone calls and tell me the truth. Why are you being rude to Shelby?"

"Ma, I don't feel like talking about it right now." I was cutting out pictures of my favorite bands from a teen music magazine. Shelby and I had started a scrapbook of cool bands over the summer. I suddenly stopped cutting because I remembered the scrapbook was at Shelby's house.

"Well, I am not going to make any more excuses for you," Ma kept at me. She began to pick up the scraps of cut paper that had fallen onto my floor.

"Fine, Ma," I said. I just wanted her to leave

me alone. I wanted everyone to leave me alone.

"You know how I hate when there are problems," Ma said as she stuffed the scraps into my little black wastepaper basket. "I'll trust you to work this one out on your own. The Andersons are good people. Shelby is a sweet girl. You wouldn't want to lose a friend like her."

"Yes, Ma."

I felt like saying, "Yeah, if you only knew how Shelby and her new friends felt about people like *us*." But I didn't.

Shelby called me three times, and all three times I asked Ma to tell her I was eating, in the bathroom, or doing homework. Each time I saw my mother's expression get angrier and angrier. I had no choice but to work things out with Shelby the next time she called.

The next time, Shelby didn't call. She came over. Ma made me come down to the door, and thank goodness, she left us alone.

Shelby's eyes were swollen from crying. I just stood in the hall and looked at her. After a few minutes of me glaring at her, and Shelby staring at her feet, she quietly said, "I think what they say is stupid. I won't go to Maryanne's party if that's the only reason why she didn't invite you, and I'll tell her why I'm not coming, too."

"Don't do me any favors," I said in the same nasty tone I had used earlier. The lump in my throat returned.

"I won't." She tried to sound just as nasty as I did.

After staring at each other for about five minutes, Shelby finally said, "I won't go, Amber, for you — and for me. They're wrong, and I know it."

I tried to look like I didn't care, but it was hard. I cared. I just wanted things to be the way they were. I wanted to go back to Deer Run Park Elementary and be happy again. Brookeville Junior High had ruined everything for us.

"I'm sorry." Shelby was about to cry again. Her lower lip started to shake, and she covered her mouth with one of her hands. I couldn't stand it any longer. I ran to her and hugged her.

"All those awful things I said — " *My* voice was shaking now, but I wouldn't let myself cry. "I didn't mean them."

Shelby hugged me back and let herself cry again. She tried to say something, but couldn't stop crying.

I couldn't stop the feeling that, even though we'd sorta made up, things would never be the same again.

16

I made sure to get to school extra early on Monday morning. No one was there, except for the teachers sitting at their desks in empty classrooms. It was funny to see Brookeville Junior High noiseless and hollow.

I didn't want to see Shelby. I hadn't talked to her since Saturday afternoon, and I was just too confused to talk to her again right now.

Just as I opened my locker to pull out the books I needed for my first few classes, Ms. West and one of last year's cheerleaders who had helped to judge Friday's tryouts walked up to Shelby's locker.

"Marcia, place one here." Ms. West was holding a sheet of paper, while Marcia held a stack of construction paper that had been cut into some kind of shape.

Ms. West looked back down at her sheet of paper and said, "This is Shelby Anderson's locker."

I had my locker opened in front of Shelby's and closed the door a little to get it out of their way. I was curious to know what they wanted with Shelby's locker.

"Thank you, Amber," Ms. West said to me, while Marcia taped one of the construction paper cutouts to Shelby's locker. Then she led Marcia to another locker farther down the hall.

SHELBY ANDERSON — Welcome to the cheerleading squad, was written on the little pom-poms. The pom-poms were made out of yellow construction paper. The words were written in bright blue Magic Marker.

Shelby had made the cheerleading squad!

After I recovered from the shock, I started feeling really jealous. I should have tried out for cheerleading, too. But I didn't want to be a cheerleader. I knew why I was jealous. I was afraid that now Shelby and Chloe would really become good friends. Maybe they would even become BEST FRIENDS. Chloe had ruined everything again!

I slammed my locker and walked away fast. I did not want to see Shelby now, not feeling the way I did. Where would I go? I had over a half hour before the bell for first period would ring. I turned down the hall and walked toward the gym. I went over to the Club Board and looked at the official listing. Why was I doing this to myself? BROOKEVILLE JUNIOR HIGH CHEERLEADING

94

SQUAD — twelve names were typed underneath. Shelby's was the first name on the list, followed by nine others. There were two names listed separately underneath: NINA BLATELY — *first captain* and CHLOE MORA — *second captain*. Of course, Chloe was a captain! I had a sickening feeling in my stomach. I wanted to go home.

Then I saw something else on the Club Board that caught my eye. LAST CHANCE TO TRY OUT FOR THE BROOKEVILLE CHORUS, the sign read. It said to stop by the music room and sign up for the last few spaces. There was still room in the chorus. Did I really have a chance to still try out? There was only one way to find out.

The music room was on the second floor, where most of the eighth- and ninth-grade classes were held. We weren't allowed to take any music classes until eighth grade, so I had never been in the music room. I peeked in. It was huge! There was a section set up for a band, with drums, amplifiers, music stands, and microphones. In another section there were pianos, a couple of guitars, and rows of seats with music stands set in front of them. They were empty now, but I could easily imagine rows of kids practicing their instruments, or singing in unison. I thought of how much fun that would be!

"May I help you?" asked a really big lady sitting at a tiny desk in the corner. I hadn't noticed her there.

"Yeah," I answered, completely surprised. "I mean, yes." I walked over to her desk.

"I wanted to know if there was still room in the chorus?" I swallowed.

"Which chorus were you interested in?" asked the big lady.

"Um, I didn't know there were two."

"Oh, yes!" answered the lady, enthusiastically. "Yes. There's the Brookeville Chorus, which is composed of up to thirty-six singers. They perform at all school assemblies and events. Their big concert is Parents' Night."

"I see." I said, trying to sound as enthusiastic as she did.

"And the Baker's Dozen is a select group of supreme vocalists who perform impromptu songs at the Christmas and spring concerts. Their big performance is the Christmas concert.

"Unfortunately," the lady continued, without taking a breath, "we had such a tremendous turnout for the chorus that we have filled our thirty-six spaces. But we are still looking for two others to complete our Baker's Dozen. Would you be interested in auditioning?"

"I sure would," I answered without hesitation.

17

I sort of made up with Shelby a couple of days after they posted the cheerleading squad list. I only managed to avoid her at school for two days.

Being a cheerleader took up twice as much of Shelby's time as trying out did. Shelby had two hours of practice every afternoon that she didn't have a game. When there was a game, she had to cheer throughout the game and then go out with "the group," which included Chloe and her friends, and some other cheerleaders. They usually went to Beverly's Ice Cream Shop, or to the mall to show off their cheerleading uniforms.

"I won't go out with the group all of the time," Shelby told me. "I just don't want them to think I'm a snob. Besides, I'm sure it would be fine if you came along."

"No, thanks." I shook my head, "I wouldn't feel right being the only non-cheerleader there." I hated the way Shelby, Chloe, and the others called themselves "the group." It was as if they were some kind of fancy club or something.

Right after her first game, and her first ice cream party with "the group," Shelby came over to my house.

"Where have you been the last few days, Amber?" she asked. "I've been worried about you. I never see you at lunch, or at the lockers in the mornings."

"I've had chorus, and I spend a lot of time practicing on my own in the music room." I tried to sound just as busy as she was. I didn't want her to think I was just waiting around for her to call or come over.

"The game was so much fun, Amber!" she cried. "Yelling, kicking, jumping, and doing splits! You should have seen how good we looked in our uniforms."

They did look cute in their uniforms. All of the cheerleaders had worn their uniforms to classes the day of the first game. I loved the blue and gold micro-mini pleated skirts, and gold sweater with the Brookeville Bear stitched on the front. They whispered to each other as they walked down the halls and gathered in groups between classes. The new cheerleaders acted like they were a clique of old friends. And of course, as Chloe had predicted, they were the main attraction for the boys.

"You should have come to the first game, Amber."

"I know, Shel, but I had to go over some music for the Baker's Dozen."

"Oh, yeah, how's that going?"

"Great! Mrs. Prudence is a great moderator. The kids are all nice — my *friend* Tamara is in the chorus, too. You remember her, don't you?" I emphasized "friend," although Tamara and I were no better friends now than we had been at the beginning of the school year.

"Yeah." Shelby nodded her head. I could tell she wanted to keep talking about the game and cheerleading.

"Amber, guess who was at Beverly's?" Shelby asked, trying to hold in her excitement.

"Who?" I asked, not as curious as she probably wanted me to be.

"P.C. — I mean, Patrick Connor!"

"He was?" I asked, surprised and suddenly interested.

"And you'll never guess what happened. Chloe walked right over to his table and started to flirt with him and his other eighth-grade friends. Then she brought them all back to join the group."

"How nice," I mumbled at the mention of Chloe and the group.

"Chloe made sure Patrick sat next to me, and he talked to me!"

"He did?"

She bobbed her head up and down. "We talked about everything — classes, the game, cheer-leading. Amber, he was so nice to me."

She leaned closer toward me and added, "I think he even likes me."

"Good," was all I managed to say. I felt so left out.

"And," Shelby continued, "he'll be at the party!"

"I thought you weren't going to the party," I demanded.

"But . . . I told him I would meet him there . . ." She paused. "I'm not going because of Maryanne, Amber. It's because of Patrick. I just want to see Patrick. What was I supposed to say when *he* asked me if I would go?"

"The truth!" I yelled. "Tell him Maryanne Sarano is a racist, and that your BEST FRIEND was not invited to her party because of it!"

"I can't do that . . . he's good friends with Maryanne Sarano. He told me that he practically grew up with her."

"So he *knows* what she is, then. That's even worse."

Shelby shrugged her shoulders. Her face turned red. "I did mention some of the things she says about bla — I mean, people from Glen View. I told him you weren't invited to the party." She was beginning to stutter nervously.

"And what did he say?"

"He . . . he . . . understood why she did it. I mean, even you know how Tamara and her friends act sometimes. . . ." She tried to choose her words carefully. She was afraid to look at me.

"No. How do they act?" I asked, sarcastically. My jaw tightened, and I felt the anger build up in my whole body, like it had that Saturday morning at Shelby's house.

"Well," she whispered, "they can be loud, and, well . . . they're just different. . . ."

"DIFFERENT? Am I different?"

"No, you're not . . . you're like me — not them."

"But I'm black, Shelby! I'm black — like THEM!"

"I know," Shelby picked at her skirt, nervously. Her hands were shaking. She stood up to my anger. "But there is a difference. Maybe because you live here, in Brookeville, and they're from Glen View. Patrick says black people are . . . well, sometimes rude, and . . . um, loud . . ." Her voice trailed off.

"He said those things?! How could you listen to him say those things about black people? Why didn't you tell him that there are loud white people, loud Asian people, and loud Hispanic people. Being black has nothing to do with being loud *or* rude."

"You aren't that way, Amber, and I told him

that. He said his family was like Maryanne's. They told him to be careful of them . . . of blacks."

"Patrick is prejudiced," I said without looking at her. "And you are, too, if you go to the party."

"I'm sorry," she told me. "I don't know what to do."

"Do what you want!" I yelled. "I don't care. You've already told me how you *really* feel."

"It's not his fault, his parents . . ." She tried to defend him, her precious Patrick *Gilbert* Connor. She was defending him, and not me!

"He's to blame just as much as his parents. He's not a baby. He has a mind of his own!"

She didn't say anything for a minute. Neither one of us said anything. Then finally she whispered, "I'll try to get out of going to the party."

We sounded like people on TV. We sounded like grown-ups. This couldn't be happening to us. I actually felt like we were on TV, acting. I wished we were.

"You have to choose, Shelby," I whispered back. "I can't be your friend anymore, not if you believe the things Patrick, Chloe, and the group believe."

She opened her mouth to say something else, then didn't. She shook her head, then got up and left. I guessed she had made up her mind.

102

18

It had been three weeks since Shelby made her decision and I went on with everything else. I spent the time catching up on my reading — I read for school, plus some reading for fun. Since we'd started school, I had managed to get four books behind in the teen series about the three high-school friends.

This weekend, Daddy and Ma decided to visit Daddy's sister, Aunt Jane, upstate. Alexandra hung out with her best friend, Betsy. They blasted music and talked on the phone for hours.

I didn't think about my problems all weekend. Why should I? They were officially over. Shelby and I weren't friends anymore. We didn't eat lunch together or wait at our lockers. She was a popular cheerleader, with a popular boyfriend . . . Patrick. She was out of my life and I tried to convince myself it was for the best. She'd made her decision the day she walked out of my room.

The Baker's Dozen had practically taken over

my life since then. I gave it my all. Mrs. Prudence even gave me a solo to sing for the Christmas concert. I practiced for the concert every afternoon, on my own.

On Sunday night, I waited for my parents to get home. The minute I heard Daddy's key turn in the lock, I ran down the stairs yelling, "DADDY! MA! DADDY! MA! WELCOME HOME!"

Later the four of us sat in the TV room and talked about our weekends. Somehow, the subject of my birthday came up. Alexandra wanted to know what I'd planned for the BIG DAY. My birthday was something I hadn't thought of since Shelby and I stopped speaking, and here it was, just two weeks away!

I was so surprised by the question, that I couldn't think of anything else to answer but, "Well, actually, I was thinking of playing it cool and just spending the day by myself."

"By yourself!" Alexandra yelled as if I had just announced I was going to swim across the Atlantic Ocean. "You aren't really going to spend the day you become a TEENAGER by yourself, are you? You should have a huge party, with dancing and boys!"

I shook my head, no. Daddy and Ma looked as shocked as Alexandra.

"You're not sick, are you?" Daddy asked, concerned.

"What is wrong, Hon? Is it because of Shelby?" Ma looked at me and waited for an answer. "I wish you would tell us what really happened to break up your friendship with her."

"I told you, she's just too busy with her cheerleading, and her friends. Besides, I've got chorus."

Shelby had ruined everything. I couldn't believe she'd let Patrick and Chloe mess up our first year of junior high. And now the best birthday of our lives was ruined, too. My thirteenth birthday was in two weeks and I was going to spend it alone.

Later, before I went to bed, Ma came into my room. I had expected her to come. I knew she was going to bring up the birthday deal again. I knew she was worried.

She sat beside me on my bed. Her eyebrows were raised and her mouth frowned. She looked at me and didn't say anything, so I said it for her.

"Ma, don't worry about me," I began. "I know you're worried because I don't want to have a big party for my birthday."

I was holding The Notebook. I was trying to decide what I was going to do with it. I didn't know if I should just throw it away, or send it to Shelby with a nasty note.

I looked down at the notebook then, and started to cry. At first, there were only tears, but then the real crying started. It was the first time I had cried in a long, long time.

Ma grabbed my shoulders and said quietly, "Oh, Amber, what's wrong, Hon? What is it?!"

I couldn't talk, so I just shook my head. I cried and cried until my head was pounding. All of my anger that I had held in since that first day of junior high, way back in September, came out in sobs. I banged my fists on the bed, then hurled The Notebook across my bedroom. This really made Ma freak.

"Tell me! Please tell me what's wrong!" she pleaded.

How could I tell her that I was crying because I missed Shelby so badly? How could I tell her why Shelby and I weren't friends anymore? How could I tell her that because I was black, I had not been invited to the biggest party of the year? How could I explain to Ma that I was having the worst year of my life!

"I just want to be treated like a person!" I yelled. "I just want to be Shelby's friend again — her BEST FRIEND!"

"So why aren't you?" Ma asked, calming herself down, then taking me into her arms. It felt really good to let it all out, there in my ma's arms.

Between sobs, I told her the whole, ugly story. I told her about Chloe, and "the group," and Maryanne Sarano and the party. I told her about Patrick, and what he had told Shelby. Ma just held me and began to cry, too.

I forced myself to stop crying, because I wanted Ma to stop.

"Sh-h-h," Ma said softly, rubbing my back. She told me she understood. She told me she suspected that someday I would have to go through this. She even blamed herself, and Daddy, for bringing up Alexandra and me in a suburb like Brookeville.

"I thought people would be better here, and wouldn't see so much of a difference," she told me. "I thought they would see my two beautiful girls, and know they were wonderful people. That's all I wanted them to see.

"But I'm sorry," she continued. "I'm so sorry you had to go through all of this. You shouldn't have to, not when you're only twelve. It's not fair that you should ever have to go through this."

I listened to her and knew she did understand. She understood everything I was going through, and she understood the things Alexandra had explained to me. I felt so relieved.

"Don't blame Shelby," Ma said. "Nobody can just turn prejudiced overnight. Not if they're smart. And I know Shelby is. It sounds as if her new friends are trying to influence her. Her friends are wrong. They're confusing her."

"She's not confused, Ma. She made a choice. She chose them."

"Shelby's been your friend for years. I don't believe she would choose people like that over you."

"She likes being popular. She likes having a boyfriend. She would choose those things over me."

Ma shook her head in disbelief. "I think you need to give her time. She'll soon realize how wrong this is. She'll realize *you* are her true friend. You'll see."

It was hard for me to believe that Shelby and I would ever be friends again. But I calmed down anyway. "Ma, why are people still racist? Why do people still have these crazy ideas?"

"I don't know, Amber, and I wish I had the answer. That's something I still don't understand, and I'm forty-six!"

"Did kids treat you like this when you were in school?"

"Well, not in school. I went to a predominantly black school in Atlanta. I guess things were a little reversed there. The white kids were the minorities. But you'd think things would have improved in, what is it, over thirty years?

"And we can't blame the kids," Ma continued. "It's the adults who put the ideas and fears into your minds."

I almost smiled. She really did understand, after all.

"What can I do, Ma? What do I do about people who are prejudiced?"

She shrugged and shook her head. "You go on living, hon. You show them any way you can that you are an intelligent human being. I'm not saying you have to go out of your way to be friends, but you show them the good person that you are and hopefully they'll see how wrong they've been."

After Ma kissed me good night and left, I wiped my eyes, which I knew must be red and scary-looking. So that was my answer. I *couldn't* do anything to change their minds. They had to change their own minds. They were wrong, and it wasn't my fault.

I really missed being Shelby's friend, and I couldn't believe she'd chosen them over me. But there was nothing I could do about it. I jumped off my bed and went to pick up the notebook I had thrown. What *was* I going to do alone on my birthday? I opened the notebook and turned to the page with our list on it. Why should I miss out on all the fun? I could do this without Shelby. I would go to New York City and spend the day alone!

Of course, Ma and Daddy wouldn't let me go by myself. But why did they have to know where I was going? I had already told them I was going to spend the day alone. I would just tell them I was going to read in the library, or shopping in the mall. I would figure out a plan!

This was becoming more exciting by the minute. This would be an adventure. A real adventure on my thirteenth birthday, and I would do it alone.

19

The morning of my thirteenth birthday, I woke up three times before I had planned. My clock was set for 6:15 in the morning, but I couldn't stay asleep.

I had the worst butterflies. I was excited about my adventure, but I also had other thoughts on my mind. I couldn't stop thinking about Shelby.

Shelby's not my friend anymore, I had to keep reminding myself. She's got another best friend now.

In my half-awake, half-asleep state, I tried to picture Shelby doing fun things with Chloe, instead of me. I just couldn't picture Chloe "creating" in the kitchen with Shelby. I kept seeing another picture in my mind. It was a picture of Shelby and me in New York City together — the two of us, like we had planned. We were running from shop to shop, trying on funky clothes, eating greasy foods from street vendors, and having a great time.

I pictured Shelby's face and big blue eyes filled with excitement. She smiled at me in the dream-like picture and said, "Anderson, I'm having the best birthday ever!" For a moment, because I was halfway dreaming, and halfway awake, I thought she was real.

"Me, too, Shelby," I said aloud. I opened my eyes, and tears poured out of them. Shelby wasn't here anymore. I was going to New York City. Alone.

" 'Bye," Shelby," I whispered, "I'll miss you."

As I lay there, I made myself feel happy for Shelby. I wanted her to be really happy. Maybe some day people like Chloe and Patrick would understand that the color I am doesn't matter at all, just the person I am inside. Maybe when I was older, I could do something to show them they were wrong.

But for now, there wasn't much I could do. It was their choice. It was Shelby's choice. I just had to make myself happy in my own way. I had to find my own friends. Maybe I could even find a boyfriend — someone as good-looking as Patrick, no, better, and a better person.

Like Ma had said, "It's just the way things are now." There were still ignorant people all over the world, but there were also a lot of good people, too. I just had to find them.

I would never forget Shelby, and all the fun we

had growing up together. It was just too bad I had to lose her to ignorance.

I squeezed the rest of the tears out of my eyes. I turned to look at my clock. The bright red digital numbers read 12:26. It was Saturday, the ninth of November. I was thirteen.

I drifted back to sleep, somehow. I woke up again at 2:40, and then again at 4:56. The next time I woke up, it was 6:38! I had less than an hour to dress and get to the bus. I raced to the bathroom to wash, then threw on my new jeans and top. Daddy and Ma would freak if they knew where I was going. I'd even bought a pair of the funky black shoes that everyone at school wore.

I grabbed my purse and the notebook and raced down the stairs, trying to keep as quiet as possible.

I was starving, but I didn't have time to eat. Luckily, it hadn't gotten too cold the night before. It had actually warmed up enough to wear just a jacket.

With only minutes to get to the bus stop, I opened the front door, and thought I heard someone in the house flush the toilet. Boy, I had to get out of there fast. My adventure was about to begin. My stomach did a flip-flop at the thought of me alone in New York City. But I ignored it.

It was still dark outside. As I walked down the

steps, my new shoes made loud clickety noises, and I prayed Ma and Daddy would not hear them.

Before I reached the bottom step, I began to hear an echo of footsteps coming down the block. The footsteps startled me, so I stopped, and held my breath. The streets were so quiet, the noise was really obvious. The steps were getting louder, and closer.

I turned to see a small figure rushing up the sidewalk toward my house.

The figure had blonde hair, was wearing what appeared to be a blue jacket, and carried a plastic shopping bag. It was Shelby!

She opened my gate and walked up to the bottom of my steps.

"I thought I had missed you," she said, out of breath, "I thought you had already left."

"How did you know I was still going?" I asked her.

"I know you, Anderson," she said with a nervous laugh.

"What are you doing here?" I asked in a plain voice.

"This is for you," she said and handed me the plastic shopping bag. I opened it and pulled out a jacket identical to the one she was wearing. On the back of the jacket *ANDERSON & ANDER-SON* was written in big white cursive letters. On the front lefthand pocket, it read in small white letters, *Amber*. Shelby pointed to the jacket she was wearing. Her lefthand pocket read, *Shelby*. She giggled.

"I quit the cheerleading team, Amber," she told me with a serious face. "It was too much work for me. I never had time for homework."

"And," she lowered her voice, "I never had time to spend with my *real* friends."

I just looked at the jacket.

"Your friend took my place on the squad — what was her name, uh, Tamara? She said something about the squad 'needing a little color added to it.' I don't really understand what she meant by that." Shelby shrugged her shoulders and smiled.

I smiled. "I think I do," I said.

"What does Chloe think about all of this?" I asked in my same plain voice. "And Patrick?"

She shrugged again, then said, "They have to accept what I want. They have to accept me the way I am. I'm *not* a cheerleader. And I *am* Amber Anderson's best friend. That is, if she'll take me back." Shelby bit her bottom lip and stared at me. I looked down at her and stared back.

"I don't understand," I said, turning the jacket over and over in my hands.

"Happy Birthday, Amber," she said.

I looked at the jacket again and said, "I didn't get you anything."

"You can buy me lunch," she said.

"Lunch?" I asked her.

She looked at her watch. "Would you come on, Anderson? We're going to miss our bus."

"*Our* bus?" I asked. "Where are *you* going?"

"With you," she said.

About the Author

Lisa Norment was born in Everett, Washington, but grew up in the suburbs of Washington, D.C. She is a recent graduate of Syracuse University, and currently resides in New York City.

Once Upon a Time in Junior High is her first book for Scholastic.

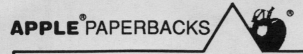